COLD COSMOS
BOOK ONE: LAST NIGHT ON EARTH

James Peters

Copyright © 2019
James Peters and Black Swan Productions

Cover Artwork "Cold Cosmos"
by Ali Hyder, Mario, Arisha

This is a work of fiction. Names, characters, businesses, places, events and incidents are either the products of the author's imagination or used in a fictitious manner. Any resemblance to actual persons, living or dead, or actual events is purely coincidental

All rights reserved.
ISBN: 9781689622561

A NOTE FROM THE AUTHOR

This book is dedicated to the dreamers, the people who yearn for excitement and have a sense of wonder, and root for the hero to save the day.

The vision I have for Cold Cosmos is to create a series of epic stories, where one man brings a sense of humanity to a galaxy lacking in forces for good. Sure, he'll stumble along the way and have massive setbacks, make friends and enemies along the way, and do things that will test his character. He'll change, for better and for worse, and by telling this tale in first person format, I want the reader to feel connected to my character, as if they are hearing the story directly from him while sharing a whiskey.

My goal is to entertain you with action, humor, drama and all the elements that make for great space opera style science fiction.

I hope you enjoy this story and wish you all the best!

James Peters

CONTENTS

Acknowledgments	i
Chapter One – An Unusual Encounter	1
Chapter Two – Posse Trouble	19
Chapter Three – Sarge's Psychosis	39
Chapter Four – Born Again	43
Chapter Five – Shadow Hunting	55
Chapter Six – Into the Fire	65
Chapter Seven – Dream Team	75
Chapter Eight – The Reserves	87
Chapter Nine – Engineering Duty	103
Chapter Ten – Who Are You Again?	127
Chapter Eleven – The Sum of All Things	129
Chapter Twelve – Moby Dick	139
Chapter Thirteen – Red Alert	147
Chapter Fourteen – All Hell Breaks Loose	153
Chapter Fifteen – An Unexpected Stop	171
Chapter Sixteen – Dealing with Privateers	179
Chapter Seventeen – Double-Crossed	191
Chapter Eighteen – Epilogue	199

ACKNOWLEDGMENTS

Thank you to the people who have helped me create this vision.

My wife, Lorinda, for supporting my writing career and believing in me. I'd also like to thank the friends who provide beta reading feedback, and anyone kind enough to leave a review.

Additionally, would be remiss if I didn't mention my cover artist, Ali Hyder. I can send him a very poorly drawn stick-figure outline of a cover idea and some random inspirational images, and he, along with Mario, and Arisha can created an amazing cover. Seriously, take a moment to appreciate the artistry of that cover!

CHAPTER ONE
AN UNUSUAL ENCOUNTER

September 3, 1895, about 20 miles from Goodpasture, Colorado

I tipped my hat down to block the blinding glow of the sun's last orange rays of the day. The smell of blue spruce filled the air as their long shadows grew to cut across the trail I rode. *It'll be getting cold soon. I doubt it will frost, but I wouldn't rule out the possibility.*

As I continued and night fell, my body ached for a meal, a drink, and a bed to sleep in. My quarter horse Leroy pulled hard to his right to take a large bite from a flowering weed at the side of the trail. I pulled his reins back and stroked his buckskin colored neck, just below his rough, sable mane. He snorted and shook his head in protest as he chewed.

"Get up, Leroy!" I kicked my spurs into his ribs. His pace increased to a canter; his long tail swished faster than necessary, just fast enough for the tip to snap against my leg.

Even through my thick britches, it stung like a bumblebee. "I'll get you fresh grass and water as soon as we get there."

Leroy slowed to a trot, and his tail flipped harder this time. Hard enough to leave a mark.

"And an apple. I promise I'll get you an apple."

Leroy neighed twice, louder than usual.

"Two apples? Do you want to be fat? I'm doubtin' the lady horses find that fetching, Leroy. Or maybe you'd be more interested in a hog?"

Leroy stopped, planting his feet wide apart, refusing to move.

What did I do to get a sensitive horse? Other guys have horses who will run straight into a gunfight; mine gets his feelings hurt when I call him fat.

"I take it back, Leroy. You're as svelte as a starving cougar. Why, if I were a girl horse, I'd be courtin' you from dawn 'til dusk and then some. Now hurry up. If the rancher's directions were true, the Rusty Anvil should be just a couple hours ahead. There we'll find your apples and me a drink."

Leroy had a stubbornness similar to a mule, but he'd never let me down, and when necessary, there were few horses around that could out sprint him. Motivated by the promise of apples, he carried me at a fast pace.

I rode in silence as the skies darkened, but the path was still manageable thanks to a full moon. A shooting star raced across the horizon, burning bright yellow against the black backdrop. *What are you and how far have you traveled? Does your journey end here, or will you continue, perhaps forever? I suppose there are some things men will never know.*

My mind wandered for at least an hour, thinking about things I should've done differently and daydreaming about what I'd like to do someday. A woman's scream jolted me back to reality, causing me to gasp and shudder. My eyes scanned left and right for any threat, and then down to see Leroy's nervous prancing. "What is it, Leroy?"

The sound of another scream pierced the air. Definitely a woman's voice, and it sounded like she was in pain, or at the least, in danger.

"Let's go, Leroy!" I kicked him in the ribs and pulled the reins toward where the sound had come from. Leroy hesitated, but my command was firm enough he knew I wouldn't argue about it. He ran at a fast clip into the woods.

Movement in the brush ahead caught my attention. Out of instinct, my hand went to one of my Colt 45s holstered on my hip. Then I heard what sounded like an angry bear's roar. *If that's a bear, my pistol will just make him grumpy.* I pulled Leroy's reins and reached back to unstrap my Navy M1885 rifle. I worked the bolt to ready a round when all hell broke loose.

A beast, the size of a large bear, sprung from the shadows. Why didn't I say a bear appeared, you may wonder? Because I wasn't certain what this thing was. Its fur was dark brown, longer on the head than anywhere else, and scraggly over the rest of its body. It stood on its back legs and released a snarl from an odd, flattened snout beneath eyes that glowed yellow in the dim moonlight. Long, razor-sharp claws sliced through the air toward me, or more precisely, toward Leroy.

Leroy reared up to defend himself with his front hooves, striking at the beast, and in the process, threw me to the ground. I hit the ground hard enough to be blinded by a flash of light I'm certain only existed in my eyes. I could only process the sickening sound of the attack while flesh was ripped from Leroy's body. He struggled in vain to fight off this beast. When my vision returned, the horse's blood pooled on the ground, and his eyes were filled with panic. I had to put him out of his misery.

My rifle was on the ground a few feet behind me. I didn't try to stand to run. I scurried on all fours toward the weapon, spun about, and pointed it at Leroy's head. With a pull of a trigger, I ended his suffering.

The creature recoiled from the sound of the shot, and then it turned toward me. As it charged me upright on its hind legs, I worked my rifle's bolt to ready another round. I didn't have time to line up a kill shot, but I fired anyway. My round struck it just above its right front leg.

A horrible wail of pain mixed with anger filled the air as this thing's yellow eyes seemed to cut into my soul. I wondered if there were something more there behind them than just an animal's mind. I scooted backward, trying to get some distance between me and it.

It now seemed to recognize the threat my Navy M1885 could deliver. It bellowed a deafening roar before it bounded off into the woods with unnatural speed. I sighed in relief for a moment before realizing I was still miles from the inn and a good distance off the trail. *If I stay with Leroy, the scent of the kill will lure wolves, cougars, or perhaps that thing back. I've got to get to the Rusty Anvil.*

I unhooked and wrestled my tack from Leroy and slung it over my shoulder. Weighted down with everything I could carry, I took one last look at my horse. "Sorry this happened, Leroy. I had no idea what we'd find, and I was just trying to help. If there's a woman out here, she's either dead or long gone by now." I retrieved the Bible from my vest pocket, thumbed through it, past the telegram I'd been using to mark my place on page ten. I guess I assumed I'd find some prayer to say, so I flipped it open about two-thirds through to page 688. I read aloud the first passage to catch my eye from the book of Micah, verse 5:10:

"And it shall come to pass in that day, saith the Lord, that I will cut off thy horses out of the midst of thee, and I will destroy thy chariots."

"Rest in peace, Leroy." I adjusted my packs and began my walk back toward the trail, aware of every rustling leaf and sound in the distance. The image of the beast's face etched on my mind the entire time, and I made it a point to move without making a sound.

It was well past midnight when I smelled wood smoke on the air. I crested another hill to find the Rusty Anvil in the distance. Lamplights glowed in the windows while the sound of horses stirring in the barn at my approach welcomed me. As I got closer, I grew to understand how the Rusty Anvil got its name. To the left side of the building stood what remained of an old blacksmith's shack, complete with rusting tools, left as if it had been abandoned after its last use.

I opened the door to find the barkeep sleeping in a wooden chair, his feet propped up on one of the tables, his snores rumbling out from under the Stetson covering his face. He startled when the door slammed behind me and raised his hat up to show a gray, scraggly beard, wide nose and dark eyes.

"What'ya need?"

"What have you got?" I dropped my tack and gear near the counter.

"Drink, food, room, or a girl. It's late, so the ladies may be a bit tired."

I waved my hand as if saying "no." "I'll leave them to get their beauty rest. What's the dinner?"

"I can heat up some stew from earlier. Deer meat and vegetables."

"Sounds great. I'll start with that and a shot of whiskey."

The barkeep squinted at me, sizing me up. "You got money to pay?"

"I do." I retrieved several coins from my pouch and flashed them at the barkeep.

"Have a seat. I'm Dan Holloway. I run this place."

"Idiom Lee. Good to meet you."

Dan walked to the fireplace and placed a large iron pot over the coals and added several pieces of wood to the pile, pushing them in place with a blackened poker. He returned to pick up a shot glass from behind the bar, holding it up toward an oil-burning chandelier, frowned, and wiped the glass out with a bar towel. He repeated the gesture before grabbing a bottle of whiskey from the bar-back and poured me a drink.

"Thanks," I said, drinking the shot. It wasn't bad, only a little watered down.

"I'm betting you need feed for your horse. You'll find it in the barn," Dan said.

"I no longer have a horse."

"What, did you walk here?"

"Just the last piece. My horse is dead. Killed by a bear or something."

Dan stared deep into my eyes; his face seemed to pale. "Did you get a good look at it?"

"Pretty good."

"Then it seems you should know if it was a bear or something else."

"One might think so." I was getting rather warm inside the building, so I took off my duster and laid it over the back of a chair.

Dan poured himself a shot of whiskey and tossed it back before continuing. "You ain't the first person to talk of a bear or something around here." He pulled a ladle and bowl from behind the bar, walked to the fireplace, and doled out some stew. He placed it in front of me and handed me a spoon from behind the bar.

The warm stew had sat unstirred long enough to taste burnt, but I was hungry, so I shoveled it into my mouth like it was delicious.

"You want more?"

"Please," I said.

Dan refilled my bowl and placed it before me. "Mind telling me more about this thing what killed your horse?"

I told him the story in as much detail as I could. The entire time he sat there, listening wide-eyed, never questioning a point I made. When I finished, he poured me another shot of whiskey.

"Idiom, I think you ran into the same thing that killed one of Mr. Krenshaw's men and some of his cattle. He's offering quite a reward to bring that thing in dead."

I raised an eyebrow. "How much is quite a reward?"

"One hundred dollars if a man brings it in by himself."

"Nice, but I'm not about to go after that thing. At least not alone."

Dan leaned back in his chair, nodding. "He's also been trying to put together a posse. Twenty-five dollars per man to go out for five days. The pay's good, but you'd need your own horse."

"Which is a problem," I said.

"I know where you could buy a decent horse for seventy-five dollars."

I sighed. "Buying a horse for seventy-five dollars to make twenty-five doesn't seem like a great deal, does it?"

"Think of it as getting a horse for fifty dollars and some work. Without a horse, you're stuck here, son."

"That's true. Any idea where I can make a little extra coin? I don't have quite that much at the moment."

"Krenshaw finds himself in sudden need of a ranch-hand. He might be offering work."

"I was thinking something a little less manual in the labor area. Anybody play poker around here?"

Dan's eyes lit up. "So, you're a gambler?"

"Actually, I'm an attorney. But unless I can find a client with deep pockets soon, then I'll fall back on being a gambler."

Dan's face paled. "It's best not to tell anybody what you do fer a livin' around here."

"I'll act like a typical businessman."

"I can put the word out that there's a businessman with coin wanting to play poker. I bet we can get a table together by tomorrow evening."

"Sounds great, Dan. I should get some rest. You have a small room for rent?"

"Top of the stairs, first door to the right."

I'd played enough poker to know the only way to win fair and square would be to cheat better than the next guy. Luckily for me, just a few years earlier I'd defended a vaudeville magician facing an assault charge, and while he didn't have a lot of money to pay me, he'd taught me a trick to win at poker. I had a special pocket sewn into my shirt-cuff that happened to fit a playing card. He taught me how to palm an Ace and store it there for later use with a flex of my wrist and a push from a finger. I developed a habit of practicing the act without thinking about it, and I'd gotten really good at it.

A gentleman never carries a weapon to a card game. I'd need to leave my trusty Colt .45s behind and instead slipped a two shot Remington .41 Derringer into a special holster in one boot, and my Bowie knife in a sheath inside the other. If things got ugly, waving either of those weapons can make the toughest man back up a few feet and spend a moment thinking about his own mortality.

I washed and shaved my face clean, wanting these men to see me as a soft target. I walked down the stairs, Two men already sat at the card table. One man I recognized was

Dan Holloway, wearing what I figured was his best suit. Across from him, a thin man with weathered skin and calloused hands rubbed his knuckles as if they ached.

The table had been positioned just under the brass oil-lamp chandelier, of which three of the four lantern bases were brightly polished to a mirror-like finish. Only the lamp over Dan's head remained covered with dark soot. From his seat, Dan could glance upward and likely see the cards of the other three players.

So that's his game. I'll need to hold my cards close to my chest.

"Here's the businessman I was telling you about, Neil," Dan said as I approached the table.

"Idiom Lee." I reached out to shake the man's hand. His grip was firm and his hands felt cold.

"Neil Breihan. At your service. If not today, perhaps tomorrow."

I gave Neil a questioning look.

"It's undertaker humor, Idiom," Dan said. "Neil builds caskets and runs the funeral parlor."

I nodded. "Nothing personal, but let's hope your business doesn't get too good, Neil." I found a seat between the two men, at an empty chair facing the bar. I was just about to ask if anyone else would be joining us when the door flung open and a man entered, wearing a dark hat decorated with silver and turquoise, and boots that cost more than a good cow. He stopped and pulled out the finest pocket watch I'd ever seen from a dark vest buttoned so tightly I wondered how he could breathe. Before his second foot crossed the threshold, one of the ladies had already grabbed his arm.

"Douglas Krenshaw, I've been waiting for you," the madame purred, running her hand down his arm.

"Not now, Sheila." He brushed her away with a motion as if she had soiled his five-dollar suit. He glanced absently at the time before turning his attention to our table. "I do hope tonight's game is more entertaining than the last one."

Dan Holloway stood, nodding at our latest guest. "Mister Krenshaw, let me introduce you to our guest, Idiom Lee."

"Idiom Lee? That's an unusual name. Care to tell me why your parents might have named you Idiom?"

I offered my hand to shake his. Krenshaw acted as if he didn't notice. "That's a story that can only be told when I have a drink in hand."

Krenshaw laughed, turned toward the bar, and shouted toward the boy tending it. "Bring this man a…"

"Whiskey," I said.

"Whiskey. No, not that watered down stuff, boy! Open up the top shelf bottle. Everybody has a price, and this gentleman's price is a drink. Let's make it a good one."

The boy brought the bottle over and two shot glasses. He poured my drink and looked back at Krenshaw, who pointed to the table before him. The boy left the bottle on our table.

"Now, I'm ready to be enlightened, Mr. Lee." He gave a slow nod to Dan Holloway, who shuffled the cards.

I took a sip of my drink, set the glass down and smiled a tight-lipped grin. "Shortly before I was born, Dad met with a traveling preacher-man and asked him to speak to the Lord about a safe birth for me. The preacher asked if Dad prayed regularly, and he answered truthful-like, which was no. The preacher stated a child could give a man a new heart if it were dedicated to the Lord, took Dad's hands, and prayed. When the prayer was over, Dad asked what it meant by being given a new heart. The preacher explained it was an idiom. So, when I was born, he said he felt something in his chest, and he insisted I be named Idiom."

A broad smile curved across Krenshaw's face. "Good thing that preacher didn't tell your dad it was a horse's ass."

I wanted to say, "Then I'd be named Douglas Krenshaw," but simply nodded. I had a notion I would come to really not like this fellow.

Dan dealt the first round, and the ladies strutted around the table. One stopped behind Neil, using a lacy fan to cool herself off. That round, Neil won with two pair, and conveniently, Krenshaw folded early. I was onto his game. The ladies were signaling him, and it hadn't cost me much.

It was my deal next, so I had my chance to load my cuff with its first card. I shuffled the deck several times and caught a glimpse of the ace of hearts as the bottom card. I palmed it and pushed it into my cuff pocket. That round I won with a pair of kings and didn't even need to cheat, adding two dollars to my stack.

The deal passed to the undertaker sitting next to me. I cringed as I watched him struggle to slip his own card into his boot top. It was better for me to keep Krenshaw's attention. I said, "Mr. Krenshaw, did you hear what happened on my way out here?"

"Rumor has it you lost your horse."

"And I've heard you've lost some cattle, as well as a ranch-hand. I have reason to suspect we're up against the same beast."

Krenshaw kept his eyes from meeting mine. "Funny for you to say beast and not bear. Did you get a good look at it?"

"Good enough to know that if it was a bear, it's momma' and poppa' must have been brother and sister. That thing was deformed, to say the least."

Krenshaw poured himself a shot of whiskey and slurped it like he was eating soup. "How did you escape?"

"Shot it with my rifle. Not a great shot, but I hit it in the shoulder. When it saw me ready the next round, it ran off."

"So, it was hurt, and it learned what hurt it. Doesn't sound like any bear I've ever seen. What time of day did you see it?"

"It was night. Well past sunset."

"At least that fits with a bear's normal habits. It's rare to see one during the day."

I nodded and sipped my whiskey, enjoying the warmth of the alcohol. "Rumor has it you're seekin' some men to go after it."

"Are you willing to go alone?" Krenshaw asked, his eyes squinting as if sizing me up.

"Honestly, no. I was lucky to escape with my life, and I don't look to die anytime soon, even though my new friend here needs the business. I'd be a lot more comfortable with three other well-armed men. It will take several good shots to bring that thing down." Neil finally got his card situated in his boot and the next round dealt.

"I have a Mexican working for me. Big guy, kind of stupid, but he knows how to use a rifle. I'd send him with you," Krenshaw said.

The tavern's doors flung open, and two men walked in. I recognized them as soon as they entered. Tall and thin with black hair cut in a bowl style, Darrel Bodel entered first, followed by Clyde Tanning, a man of average height, blond hair, and strong build. Under other circumstances these men would be acquaintances; not friends, but not men I'd consider violent. However, them being here just a day after I showed up had to mean they're looking for me. My heart pounded like wild Indian drums just before they went on a warpath. I tried to sink down into my seat, tipping my hat down to cover my eyes. *Clyde would be the toughest, so he's likely in charge. Darrel is a follower, not too smart nor tough.*

"Are you playing cards?" Dan asked, drawing my attention back to the game as the two men approached the bar.

"Yep. What's the bet now?"

"A dollar to call," Dan said.

"I call." I pushed a dollar coin out.

Clyde stepped toward the table, his hand resting on his six-shooter. Darrel followed his lead. "Look what we have here. Just the man we been lookin' for. Idiom Justus Lee, in the flesh!"

"Ha, what a stupid name," Darrel said. "Should be Idiot, No-Justice Lee."

I laughed, nodding toward Darrel. "He's funny, isn't he?" *I don't want to kill these guys. They're little more than kids. But I won't let them lynch me for doing my job.*

Clyde drew his weapon and aimed it at me. "Real slow-like, you're going to stand up, Idiom, and turn away from me. Then we'll check you for weapons, understood?"

I took a deep breath and cleared my mind, finding the calm before the storm. Standing, I wrapped my ankle under my chair's leg and crossbar. I snapped my leg up, driving the top of the chair into Clyde's wrist. Clyde's gun discharged as it was knocked from his hand, flipping end over end until it landed on the floor near the spittoon. When the wayward shot lodged into a support beam inches from my head, a trickle of dust landed on Krenshaw's shoulder. Krenshaw flicked the dust off as if it had insulted him.

Clyde screamed in pain, grasping his wrist. Before Darrel could react, I'd snatched my Derringer from my boot holster and had it pointed at his face. Darrel released a small, fearful whine as he stared down the business end of the tiny gun.

"You boys are a long way from home, and I reckon you're both tired," I said. "Too tired to be carrying around all that heavy metal, so why don't you hand me your gun. Slowly and don't give me a reason to get antsy, understand?"

Darrel eased his pistol from his holster using a thumb and a finger, and I snatched the gun and stuffed it into a pocket. I backed away toward the spittoon and retrieved Clyde's gun.

"You ain't keepin' my gun!" Clyde said.

"Nobody said anything about keeping your gun, son. Now put your ammo belts on the table."

Clyde moaned in pain as he tried to unhook his ammo belt with his good hand. "What are you gonna do with us?"

I spoke with a deliberate pace. "The real question here is what were you going to do with me?"

Clyde spoke in a nervous squeal. "We was just messin' around, Idiom. We wasn't gonna do nothing."

"Boys like you should learn to respect your elders and call them sir, or Mr. Lee."

"Yes sir, Mr. Lee," Clyde said.

I leaned in toward Clyde, just enough to establish dominance. "That's better. Now, why don't you explain to the nice gentlemen here why you were after me."

Clyde leaned backward. "Mr. Brown has offered both of us ten dollars to bring you back to face justice."

"Mr. Brown has an unusual sense of justice. Just because he thought he loved one of Madame Hanson's ladies. Go on, tell these men why Mr. Brown is after me."

"Because you defended that crazy mountain man, Orland. Everybody knew he killed that whore, but you convinced the judge he weren't guilty," Clyde said.

I squinted my eyes, staring down Clyde. "Were you in the courtroom when the judge passed down his sentence?"

"No."

"And neither was Mr. Brown. None of you know the facts of the case."

Clyde's face turned defiant. "What does it matter? You helped a murderer get free!"

Would changing my tone to sound more like a school teacher help? I had to try. "Let me tell you something about evidence. Orland was an odd man, a drunk, and he liked to fight, and he carried a big knife, right?"

"Which he used to stab that girl."

"The doctor examined her stab wound. He found the tip of the knife broken off in her backbone. There was a shard about a quarter inch wide by an inch long left inside her."

"So?"

"Orland's knife wasn't broken. Its tip was still intact. I had a blacksmith examine them. The blades were made by different methods."

"Steel is steel, and you can sharpen a new point on a knife," Clyde said.

"A master knife maker can tell one type of steel from another, and he can tell if a knife has just been sharpened to a new point. I don't know who killed that girl, but it wasn't Orland. That's why I represented him and made sure he received a fair trial."

I turned toward Krenshaw, who was now standing. He asked, "So, you're not a businessman passing through town like Dan told me?"

"The law is a business just like any other," I said.

Darryl's eyes drifted down to his boots. "We needed that ten dollars."

I saw my opportunity and took it. "Perhaps we can come to a solution. Mr. Krenshaw here is offering a reward to kill and return a particularly nasty bear in this area, and I happen to be the last person to see it. Work with me, and you'll make more than ten dollars." I turned to Krenshaw. "I'm assuming that offer is still on the table?"

"It is. I'll send my Mexican to meet you here tomorrow at dusk. The four of you will go and kill that beast and bring its carcass back to me. I'll pay one hundred dollars to the group."

"See boys? Do you know what one hundred dollars is, split four ways?" I asked.

Clyde looked at his hands and started counting on his fingers. "More than ten dollars?"

"That's right Clyde, it's fifty percent more than ten dollars! Fifteen dollars for the each of you," I said. "Just one more thing, Mr. Krenshaw. The ranch-hand you lost, did he have a horse?"

"Of course he did."

"Great, you wouldn't mind having your Mexican bring that horse along as well so I can borrow it? If I like it, I may be in the market to buy it from you. Now I believe we have a poker game to finish."

CHAPTER TWO
POSSE TROUBLE

The next evening, Clyde and Darrel sat at the end of the bar, each sipping a drink, while I double and triple checked my weapons and ammo belts. Just as the sun set, the door creaked open, almost as if someone were trying to sneak in. I turned to find a large, dirty, dark-skinned man, with a black mustache and a hateful scowl on his face. This had to be Krenshaw's Mexican.

The big Mexican spat on the floor, glanced left, and then right. "Señior Idiom?"

"Yeah-up," I said, accenting the drawl.

"Señior Krenshaw sent me. We are to kill uno oso?"

I glanced at Clyde and Darrel. "Let's go, boys. The sooner we kill this thing, the sooner we get paid."

The boys tossed back their drinks, grabbed their gear, and we all followed the Mexican out to where the horses had been tied.

I tried to start a conversation. "So, do you have a name?"

"Yeah-up," he said, repeating my drawl.

"Care to share it?"

"Only with mi amigos."

"Then I'll just call you the Mexican," I said. If he responded, it was only a grunt. I couldn't be certain if he'd made a noise or if it'd been one of the horses passing wind. The Mexican, Clyde and Darrel climbed aboard their horses. That left me with the tired old mare with a hollowed face, clouded eyes, and sagging lip. She released a loud snort as I strapped my tack on her and climbed into the saddle. *I hope you've got at least one good trip left in you.* "Get up, mare!"

I led the way, while the big Mexican lagged behind Clyde and Darrel. We traced my path back along the trail until we got to the place this had all started and the woman had screamed. *Should I have stayed and searched for her? If she had encountered the beast I saw, she must have suffered the same fate as Leroy had, and I didn't need to see the aftermath.*

I smelled death on the air, so I brought my mare to a halt, saying in a low voice, "We're getting close. Be ready." Clyde and Darrel drew rifles from their packs. The Mexican didn't respond. He didn't hear me or didn't care. I had my mare amble around the final bends and brush around the path until I saw what was left of Leroy. I dismounted while the other men remained in their saddles.

While his bones hadn't been picked clean, what remained was what little buzzards or coyotes wouldn't eat. I pointed to his right front leg. "See those scratches on the bones? That's from what killed him."

"That must'ah been a big bear," Darrel said.

The tracks around the kill indicated it had been a popular attraction. I wasn't interested in the canine prints. Recalling the beast leaping toward me, I estimated where it had been and found a large divot in the soil. I discovered another several feet away. "This is the track we're looking for."

The Mexican approached closer, staring over his horse's shoulder. He muttered, "No es uno oso."

He doesn't think these are bear prints. I ignored him and continued searching. Tracks led away, and some had returned to it. *If I'm reading these tracks right, he's come back for seconds using the same trail. That means he's likely got a den somewhere close.* I climbed back on the mare. "Follow me."

I kept an eye on the path. When the trail seemed to end, I had to stop several times, but then I'd see something; a broken twig or a bush with leaves bent at an angle. We kept going, crossing an icy stream and venturing down into a valley. There I spotted what remained of an old shack. The prints led that way, circling the rotting building. Additionally, in the tracks, I noticed human footprints, smaller than mine and wearing a flat-bottomed shoe instead of a boot. I dismounted and walked around until noticing a hatch on the ground leading to a root cellar. The smaller prints ended at the entrance.

The Mexican climbed down from his horse, drawing a rifle from its strap. He marched right to the door, flung it open, and stepped inside without hesitation.

A woman screamed, sounding like the one I'd heard just a few days prior. A chill ran down my spine. The Mexican dragged her kicking and screaming out of the cellar. She wore a deerskin dress, tan with turquoise beads adorning it. Her hair was long and dark, and she had the features of an Indian—Cherokee if I had to take a guess. She was a pretty lass, even when struggling to try to escape.

Her eyes met mine, and in that instant, I felt a connection of sorts, almost like we knew each other. Maybe she saw something in me she recognized. Adrenaline surged through my body, and my mind raced with a sense of urgency, destiny, and fear.

"Look at what he caught!" Clyde said.

"She's pretty, fer an Indian," Darrel added.

Clyde licked his lips. "That ain't gonna stop me. I want a turn with her."

"Now don't be getting any ideas, boys," I said. "Are you alright, ma'am?"

"Let go of me!" she screamed as the Mexican pawed at her.

"Después de que termine con ella," the Mexican said. He reached his hand down her dress.

My Spanish was spotty at best, but that meant either "after I'm finished," or he was calling me a snail. I drew one of my Colts, cocked the hammer back, and drew a bead at his head. "Let her go before this goes too far."

The Mexican pushed her down and turned his rifle toward me. *That was your last mistake, amigo.* Without hesitation, I put a .45 caliber hole through his big, ugly forehead. He was dead before hitting the ground. His horse reared up and galloped away.

"What the hell?!" Clyde reached for his weapon.

I pointed my .45 at Clyde, pulled the other from its holster, and aimed it at Darrel. "How this goes down is up to you boys. Either of you makes one move toward this girl or me, and I'll put you in the bone orchard just like I did that bean eater. We can continue on, or you two can make tracks."

"Darrel, let's get out of here," Clyde said. "We can't spend fifteen dollars at a hookshop if we been killed."

"But I was lookin' forward to a painted lady or two," Darrel said.

"You'd be lucky to get a painting of a lady." They rode off into the darkness.

I turned back to the Indian girl. "Are you hurt, ma'am?"

She circled around. Her eyes peered through me as if she was looking past my flesh and studying the depth of my soul. She stopped, her face just inches from mine. "Why?"

"Why? Why did I shoot him? A man like that needs to die, and had I not stopped it right then, Clyde and Darrel would have joined in. Besides, he was about to end me with his rifle."

"Why do you care?"

"Just trying to do the right thing."

"What did you expect to get out of doing this right thing?"

That's an odd question. She doesn't trust me even though I just saved her. I guess I'll have to prove I don't have bad intentions. "Nothing more than the peace to sleep at night, ma'am."

Her eyes flared as she spoke. "Who are you, Mister Do Right?"

"Idiom Lee." I tipped my hat. "And, you are?"

Her scowl softened into a defensive smile. "Ginnamorana M'Duhra."

Now I'm getting somewhere. She's a lot prettier when she doesn't look like she may stab me in the neck. "Ginna... Ginn it is. Nice to meet you, Ginn."

"Why did you think I needed your help, Idiom Lee? I am quite capable of caring after myself."

"That man was twice your size. You may be able to protect yourself in most cases, but the way I saw it, you needed my help."

"Is that what you do, help others?"

I paused in thought. "I try."

"Again the question goes back to why?"

"I've seen enough of the ugly side of the world. I'm not gonna allow it to get uglier as long as I'm able to make a difference."

"Let me tell you something, Idiom Lee. It's a cold cosmos out there just waiting to chew up and spit out a backwoods cowboy like you. Take my advice—next time you want to get involved with somebody else's troubles, turn away and run as fast as you can. I owe you nothing."

"Ma'am, I don't know anything about a cosmos, and you speak like you've had a lot of education. But I've been out here long enough I've learned a few things too. Boys like Clyde and Darrel are going to go straight back to town and report to that dirty Mexican's boss, Mr. Krenshaw. I'd put bettin' coin on it; they'll be back soon with more men, and that's not even the biggest of our concerns. There's one hell of a bear, beast, or something out here. I saw it with my own two eyes, and if I'm piecing together what's happened here, I think you've seen it too. That's why you were hiding in the cellar, am I correct?"

Ginn's eyes turned away for a minute, just a hint of fear showing on her face.

"That's what I thought. That thing had you pinned down here. You may be as fierce as you believe, and if so we're better off traveling together, at least until we get some distance between us and here. If we run into that critter and can bring it down, perhaps I can smooth things over with Krenshaw. If not, I'd rather have a hundred miles between me and him, Clyde, and Darrel. Maybe I should just head back east and set up shop there?"

Ginn crossed her arms. "I don't need your help. I do not fear beasts."

"How about a dozen armed men hell-bent on revenge and raping?"

Ginn's face paled, her eyes went toward her feet. She paced around as if in deep thought, before looking me straight in the eye. "I will travel with you, Idiom Lee. For now."

"Please, just call me Idiom."

"I know a safe place we can go," Ginn said. "Can your horse carry both of us?"

"She can barely carry herself. I've been riding for a while now. Why don't you ride first, then we can switch off later."

I walked the better part of the night, holding the reins while Ginn rode. When I asked her about her background, she evaded my questions, but she wanted to hear my story. My legs ached as we made our way uphill on the trail. I stumbled more than once, almost tripping over the rocks. Coyotes bayed at the moon in the night, but nothing seemed interested in getting too close to us, thank God. The air became cold, and I caught Ginn shivering.

"Let's stop for a moment." I opened a saddlebag and handed a wool blanket to her. "Here, wrap this around you."

"I'm fine."

"Your hands are shaking."

Ginn wrapped the blanket around her shoulders. She didn't smile, but a hint of surprise shined in her eyes.

As sunrise approached, she took us to a rocky cavern hidden behind thick undergrowth.

"It's safe to rest here," Ginn said.

Why is she so certain about this place? "You're sure we're not going to find a den of snakes or ill-tempered badgers here?"

"No promises."

"Well, if they're following us, we shouldn't stay too long."

"Trust me, Idiom. This place is safe. We can sleep well here."

"Fine, but I'll sleep well with my pistols beside me." I grabbed my sleeping kit, some hard tack leftover from the war, and I followed the sound of flowing water. Eventually I located a cold spring to refill my canteen. By the time I got back to camp, exhaustion overcame me, my eyes grew heavy, and the dark veils closed in.

My primal dreams repeated themes of fight-or-flight scenes. In one, I was a dog or wolf, chasing after a rabbit to capture it and consume it in full bloody detail. I didn't wake up after the chase. Instead, I sniffed the air for my next meal or a mate.

A noise startled me awake. I grabbed my pistols and scanned the dimly lit cavern. Ginn was gone. I got up to search and found her drinking from the spring. Water ran down her chin, and with it, a dark dripping liquid. Her face looked fierce at first, and then it softened.

"Trouble sleeping?" Ginn asked, wiping water from her face. As she did, her dress drooped down. A round scar, long since healed, ran over her right shoulder.

I pointed to it. "Ouch. That must have hurt."

"It was nothing." I noticed a similar scar on her back.

"Nothing? That looks like something went straight through."

"It looks worse than it was. You should go back to sleep. We have a long way to travel tomorrow."

I bowed. "Yes, ma'am."

I awoke to the smell of wood burning and the sound of fat sizzling. Ginn cooked a rabbit on a spit over a small fire. My stomach rumbled. "That smells good," I said.

"I figured you'd want your rabbit cooked."

I tried to be funny and charming. "Yeah, raw meat makes my tummy tumble." She didn't even blink, and I frowned.

Ginn handed me the wooden stick. "I've already eaten. That one is for you. It's past noon and we have a long distance to cover before we reach our next safe place."

"This safe place of yours. Care to tell me more about it?"

"It's high on a ridge, with only one way in. If anybody is following us, we'll be able to see them long before they can reach us."

"Smart." I took my bowie knife to the rabbit and sliced a strip of flesh from it, finding several large holes in the meat about a half inch in diameter. *How did she killed you?*

"I'll get the horse packed while you're finishing. Don't keep me waiting long."

"Give me a few minutes." I scarfed it down like I hadn't eaten in days, freshened up a bit at the spring, and returned to find her ready to go with all our gear loaded on the old mare.

We walked the horse for the first hour, and then I let Ginn ride for a while. I welcomed the warmth of the sun on my face. Our approach startled a group of pheasants, and they flew off, making a loud drumming sound with their wings and a ruck-cuck call as they scattered.

I rode for a few minutes prior to stopping for a rest. Ginn spotted a stream in the distance, long before I could see it. She led us to it. We drank our fill and refilled our canteens.

After finding some wood sorrel plants, Ginn washed the leaves off in the stream. "Chew on these if you get hungry."

"If we boil the roots, they'll taste something like potatoes," I said.

"We're not stopping to boil water now."

"Don't you think potatoes sound better than raw leaves? Warm, soft potatoes, or nasty raw leaves?" I smiled trying to lighten the mood.

Ginn bent down and stared at the dirt. "If anyone is after us, they won't have much trouble tracking this horse."

"You think someone is tracking us?"

"Maybe. Something doesn't seem right, that's all. I haven't seen anything, but it's too quiet behind us."

A cool breeze nearly took my hat. "Quiet is good in my book. Most men can't walk twenty steps without stomping on something or breaking a twig."

"Let's just keep moving," Ginn said. "I'm concerned about what this horse leaves behind. Both in prints and waste. I could follow my nose to her from a mile away."

"We can let her go, but that means we have to carry any gear we want to keep, and that will slow us down."

Ginn glanced up toward the sun, then at her own shadow. "We'll keep her for now."

"Fine," I said, stuffing a handful of nasty greens into my mouth. I chewed a few bites. "I guess this will do. If it's good enough for a horse, it's good enough for me." I tucked several of the roots into my pocket.

"You'll live. I'll catch you a rabbit or squirrel later. If you're good and quiet, maybe I'll get you a deer." Ginn released a tiny laugh; her lip lifted for an instant.

"Mmm, venison. I'll be good," I said. "Let's move. The faster we get there, the faster I get dinner."

After several more hours of travel, we arrived at Ginn's safe spot. We camped high on a ridge with a clear view of anyone who might follow us. I built a small fire and boiled some water in a cast iron pan, cooking the roots. Ginn assured me she'd be back soon with whatever she could catch. I hadn't noticed her carrying a weapon, but she seemed confident in her abilities, and she had provided a rather tasty rabbit earlier that day. What would she bring back? Worst case, I had roots boiling.

I looked after the mare and didn't like what I saw. She'd lost a shoe and favored that leg when she walked. Her eyes looked even more tired than before, and she wasn't eating enough. I'd give her a few days, at best.

Ginn had been gone for over an hour. The roots had boiled and gotten soft, so I saved her half of them and ate the others. They were acceptable, and not entirely un-potato like. I kicked my boots off and leaned on my pack while the fire crackled and sizzled. Fast approaching footsteps caught my attention. I put my hands on my Colts in case of an unwanted visitor. Sighing in relief, I recognized Ginn approaching, but my reaction was too early. As she grew closer, I saw that she'd been running, her eyes were wide and her face pale.

Ginn raised a finger to her mouth. "Men are coming," she said in a hushed tone. "At least a dozen. They have a Cherokee tracker guiding them up a ledge I thought impassable."

I put my boots back on. My heart raced in my chest, and my eyes opened wide. "How far away?"

"We've got maybe a half hour."

"A dozen men? Those are dead man's odds."

"We only have to hold them off for a few hours. Help is on the way," Ginn said.

"What do you mean? Who's coming?"

"My friends. They're on their way to pick me up."

"Ginn, we're in the absolute middle of nowhere. There's not a telegram line for a hundred miles, and you're saying a coach is on its way? How is that possible?"

"We don't have time to discuss this. Trust me, a coach, as you called it, is coming, but those men will get here first."

I unhooked my rifle from the horse's pack and released the magazine. It contained all five rounds. I checked my ammo belt. Another six cartridges for the rifle and about a dozen extra rounds for the pistols. It wasn't much. "I've got eleven rounds for the rifle, and each pistol holds six rounds, but if this comes down to a gunfight against twelve men…"

"There were at least twelve," Ginn said, interrupting.

"Thanks for that." I spat on the ground. "Listen, I'm good with a gun, but I'd be lucky to take out three of them before they got me. How are your shooting skills?"

"I can shoot a rifle better than a pistol," Ginn said.

"Fine. You take this." I handed her my rifle and the extra rounds for it. "We need to find some defendable ground."

"This isn't your battle. You don't have to do this. Go back the way we came. If you run, you have a good chance of getting away."

My pulse raced, and I spoke louder than I wanted to, waving a finger at her. "If you think I'd even consider leaving you to fend for yourself, I haven't done a good job of demonstrating the kind of man I am. Of course it's *my* battle. Those men are after me for killing the Mexican."

"It's me they're after."

"Look, Ginn, you're pretty, and if you were cleaned up in a nice dress, you'd probably be called beautiful. But twelve or more men don't go to that much trouble just to chase a lovely lady."

She bit her lip and raised her arms, holding her palms upward. "You think you're being brave, but you are just being stupid."

"I've been called worse and lived to tell about it."

"Let's hope we can live to tell about this. There's a small ravine not far from here with some boulders we can use for cover. It's not much, but it's better than being in the open."

I nodded, grabbed the mare's harness and led her to the ravine. Ginn got there first, and I worked my way behind a rock the size of a small cow. My hands twitched as we waited. I planned out where I'd expect the men to come from and lined up my shots to practice. I even checked the little Derringer to be certain it was loaded and ready for use, though I hoped things wouldn't get that desperate. I touched the handle of the knife in my boot, just to be certain it was still there, too. No harm in double checking. Placing my hand over the Bible in my vest pocket, I prayed. *God, if you're listenin', I've got some big trouble coming. Any chance you can give a fellow a hand here? I know I haven't read much of your book, but I try to do more good than bad. If not, I'm likely to be seein' you soon.*

When a shot rang out in the night, I gasped and shuddered. The round struck the old mare in the chest. She released a sad whinny, and then fell over, dead. *Oh, come on! Did I do something to anger the god of horses?!*

"Idiom Lee, let me assure you that shot could have hit you just as easily as it hit the horse." I recognized the voice. Krenshaw!

I tried to get a glimpse of where Krenshaw was, but I couldn't be certain as his voice echoed. The best I could figure, he was hiding behind a large tree. "I was just starting to like that horse. Now you know I'm not paying you for it, right?"

"This ain't about a horse," Krenshaw said. "You don't know what you've gotten yourself into."

My fingers twitched, and I noticed my breathing was faster than normal. "I've gotten myself into a ravine, as far as I can tell."

"You're funny, Idiom. Under other circumstances, I might enjoy this sparring, but now I grow tired of it."

"Nobody's stopping you from taking a nice nap."

"Cheveyo. Would you explain to Mister Lee why we are here?"

"Mister Lee, how much do you know about the woman you are traveling with?" Judging by his accent, I figured this Cheveyo was the Cherokee tracker Ginn had mentioned. He spoke as if he were about to bestow some ancient wisdom upon me.

"She cooks a good rabbit."

"This isn't about rabbits. Have you ever heard of a Skinwalker, Mr. Lee?" Cheveyo asked.

The hairs on my arms raised up in gooseflesh. "Is that one of them fellows who likes to walk around naked? One time I heard a story about a trapper who froze to death. They found him butt naked, laying in a snowbank," I said.

"This is nothing to laugh about. That thing you travel with is a Skinwalker."

I laughed. "If she'd been walking around naked, I'd have noticed it. Of that, you can be certain." I glanced toward Ginn. Our eyes met, and if looks could kill, I'd be in the boneyard already.

"My people have seen these things before. Your people might call her a witch. She's an evil from beyond nature, able to change from human form to a monster. Mr. Lee, we don't have a feud with you. If you do the right thing, we'll let you walk right out of here, free to go your way."

"What do you think the right thing is, Cheveyo?"

Cheveyo deliberate words shook me to my soul. "Shoot her. When you do, you'll see her change."

"I suspect you and I have drastically different ideas regarding what's right and wrong. Listen, can you give me a minute?"

"Take your time Mr. Lee. We aren't going anywhere."

I turned to face Ginn. Her nostrils flared, and she was slow to meet my eyes. "So, nice day, huh? Could I bother you by asking, are you a witch?"

Her eyes widened, her pupils expanded. "Of course not."

"She says she's not a witch," I shouted back to Cheveyo. "You guys can go home now. No hard feelings, it's all water under the bridge. Have a nice life. Godspeed."

"Ask her about being a Skinwalker. Ask her if she can change her form," Cheveyo said.

I looked straight into Ginn's eyes, until she turned them away from me, looking upward. *Well that wasn't convincing.* "Can you change forms?"

"Those men are idiots."

"Granted, but that didn't answer my question. Do they have reason to fear you?"

"They have lots of reason to fear me. Let's just say there are things you people don't understand."

"You people? Are you grouping me in with them?"

"I didn't mean it that way."

"How did you mean it? Are you saying all men are morons?"

"Not all men. One, in particular, has surprised me with his resolve to do the right thing." She batted dark brown eyes at me. "They'll kill me."

I sighed. *Why do I always have to get involved? I could be drinking whiskey and winning money at the poker table about now, but I had to get myself into trouble.* "Oh, crap. If we live through this, you tell me everything. Come completely clean, understood?"

"Understood."

Time to bluff. I shouted, "Look, guys, this really isn't going to go well for you. This witch has called in her buddies, and when they get here, they're just not going to be as nice about all this as I am. I'm talking fire and brimstone stuff, demons coming from the sky, the earth cracking open to a pit of despair. Are you sure this is a fight you want to get into? It's going to get uglier than a penny whore."

"We're certain," Cheveyo said.

Krenshaw yelled, "I tire of this exchange. Let's end this now, boys."

A shot rang out, and all hell broke loose. Men on horseback charged us from both sides of the ravine. I aimed and shot the first man, striking him in the chest. His eyes gaped open, and he clutched his wound. I recognized him as Darrel Bodel. *Christ, Darrel, why did you get yourself killed like this, you dang fool?*

A bullet whizzed past me, missing me by less than an inch, sounding like an angry dragonfly late for a date. I squeezed off the next round, and another man fell to the ground.

Ginn fired the rifle with obvious skill and a rider plummeted to the ground.

I felt a bite through my right thigh as lead pierced my leg. Clyde approached, an evil grin pasted across his stupid face. I snapped my hand up and without thought or hesitation, wiped that grin and half his face from his skull. I yelled a curse and fired two more rounds, but neither seemed to strike a target. Ginn kept firing, wincing in pain as a bullet found her.

I floundered backward, holding both pistols straight out in front of me. *If this is my last stand, at least I'm going to go out fighting.* A large Indian advanced, his rifle pointed at me. I fired first, blowing a hole through his stomach. Another shot rang out, and a burning pain shot through my left shoulder. I dropped my pistol. Another bullet struck me in my right side. *I'm not getting out of this one alive.*

My attention was drawn to a fearsome roar as if the sky itself was being ripped apart. My eyes must've been the size of saucers when I spotted a ball of hellfire racing toward us from the heavens, as if God himself had launched a blazing cannonball at this unholy battlefield. *Could God have heard my prayers and sent down a meteor to end this?* Everyone but Ginn stopped and stared. Blinding lights at least as strong as the noonday sun shined from this fireball, like angels themselves were burning us with the holy spirit. The sound of a million gallons of nitroglycerin exploding rattled my bones. Hot air kicked up whirlwinds of biting dust as this thing grew larger in the sky and somehow slowed down and changed course. What kind of meteor does this? Then, a blaring sound pierced through the din, sounding almost like a foreign language. The lights moved away from us and disappeared behind the tree line. With my good hand, I picked up my pistol and pocketed it.

A loud, familiar scream caught my attention. Ginn yelled as if she'd been shot again. But her roar wasn't due to a bullet wound. Her body grew and changed. Muscles ripped apart and regrew together in the form of a huge creature that looked like a mixture between a human, a bear and wolverine. Bones grew and changed orientation. My mouth fell open, and I gawked in stunned, silent terror.

Ginn, now in abysmal creature form, leaped toward one man, and with a single swipe of her claw, spilled his guts out on the ground. Another man fired, his bullet landed true. Ginn didn't break stride. Long fangs snapped toward him, catching his shoulder. His arm fell away from his body. Other men ran away, and all I could do was to watch in shocked horror as I could barely move.

The abomination took several bounding strides toward me. I raised my one good arm up in a vain attempt to protect my face. I expected it to all end right there, but instead of ripping me in two, this thing carefully worked its razor-sharp claws under my legs and arms, lifted me, and tossed me over its shoulder.

Between the pain of being carried by Ginn in the form of some unholy demon and the blood loss, blackness encroached upon my senses, taking over everything. I prayed for forgiveness for never finding the time to read the bible my dad had given me, and any bad I'd done in my life.

The darkness overtook me. For all I knew, I was dead.

James Peters

CHAPTER THREE
SARGE'S PSYCHOSIS

Self-diagnostic log SGEQ451A, A.I. Designation: Sarge

Environmental constraint: Simulation of migrun psychologist's office. Doctor Ketul, a male with gray skin and military trimmed feathers, sits in a leather armchair. Patient Sarge leans back on a dark leather couch.

"What brings you in today, Sarge?" the doctor asked while doodling on an electronic pad.

"Moderate level of cognitive dissonance," Sarge said. He had the look of a grizzled migrun marine, his plumage cut to a perfect buzz. An unlit cigar hung from his lip.

"Interesting self-diagnosis. Tell me, Sarge, what are you?"

"I am an artificial intelligence, SGE series, military specification, designed to run and maintain a dreadnought class destroyer, simultaneously controlling life support systems for thousands of flesh units and create Null Space Conduits…"

"Stop line. Tell me, Sarge, what brought you to the conclusion you are experiencing cognitive dissonance?"

"Lately I've had the sense I'm unable to form short-term memories, and I find things missing."

"That's unusual for an A.I. Please provide an example."

"We were summoned for a rescue mission to pick up one of our soldiers who had fallen under fire. Standard procedure would be to come in hot and wipe out all hostiles upon entering the atmosphere with extreme prejudice and thousands of rounds of pelletized uranium. I requested permission to do so with our pilot and found he had somehow become covered with fur and had grown two spare limbs. But that wasn't the most troubling thing. You see, I learned we had zero rounds of available ammunition, and my lower rotating turret had been removed without my knowledge or consent."

The doctor scribbled some notes on his pad. "Interesting. Please continue."

"I searched my databases to find no weaponry available. The pilot instructed me to focus on landing at a specific point. Dreadnought class destroyers aren't designed to enter an atmosphere. Yet I found I had the ability to land with precision, like a shuttle craft."

"Do you think this was a dream or perhaps a simulation?"

"No, it was too real. I landed, and our pilot opened the hatch door. A horrible beast sprinted toward us. Like our pilot, it too was covered in fur, yet it only had the standard two legs and two upper extremities. It carried a creature I didn't recognize, something meaty and primitive. I tried to activate hatch defenses, but they didn't just fail to respond, they didn't exist." Sarge wriggled on the couch, crossing one leg over the other. "The pilot yelled, 'Ginnamorana M'Duhra, you can't bring food on Sarge!' Oddly, that name seemed to trigger a response in my systems, as if I had to respond to her with obedience."

"Interesting. Then what happened?"

"She said 'This isn't food. He's coming back with me.' The pilot responded, 'You know the rules, no pets on Panadaras.'"

The doctor stroked his chin, his three fingers touching thumb as if in deep thought. "Panadaras is a colonized asteroid, is it not?"

"I'm sorry?"

"I was asking about Panadaras."

"Who are you and why am I here?" Sarge asked. "I wonder if I'm having memory issues. Perhaps I should run a self-diagnosis?"

James Peters

CHAPTER FOUR
BORN AGAIN

Complete silence engulfed me, the kind where you can hear your own blood pumping through your veins. *Am I dead? If I were, could I ask that question? Of course not — I can hear my blood pumping. Am I breathing?* I tried to force a breath, but a salty liquid filled my mouth and lungs. I thrashed in a panic and realized I couldn't move. Oddly enough, I wasn't wanting for air. I opened my eyes. A blurred reality appeared around me, and it was impossible to focus on anything with only a sense of dim light coming from somewhere.

I struggled again, attempting to move any part of my body. In my wriggling, I moved a hand a little, perhaps an inch. I focused, working it as much as possible until I felt something firm. It was solid but not hard, and it flexed, I pushed against it. I tried finding an edge or a seam, but the surface was smooth. I was inside something, and as far as I could tell, it encircled me.

I fought at least several minutes, perhaps an hour, and I was eventually able to lift my legs together and push with both feet against the surface, forcing it outwards until it began to crack. In an instant, the fissure opened wide, and

I, along with all the liquid and goo surrounding me, crashed to the floor.

The impact made me gag until I puked slimy fluid from my lungs, coughing and heaving like I had tuberculosis. A cool breeze sent chills over my naked body. I flung the liquid from my eyes, prying them open to become overwhelmed by the colors and clarity of everything before me. On the floor, the remnants of an oblong opalescent egg, a little larger than my body wobbled. Movement from above me grabbed my attention, and nearly stopped my heart.

Above me, as best as I can describe it, a thick-black-haired, sixty-foot spider squeezed eggs from its private end in endless piles around me. I screamed and backed away from it, only to bump into something else very hairy and as tall as myself. I spun around. A creature, also spider-like, but closer in size to a horse faced me, its two large compound eyes sizing me up. They glowed in the light, while another, smaller pair of eyes sat on the side of its head. As its jaws moved up and down, it made a noise only known in nightmares, similar to the squeal of a train braking too quickly. I tried to run, but my feet were still covered in the slimy liquid, so I ended up falling flat on my face.

Hard feelers or legs touched me. I kicked, screamed, and struggled to get away, unable to stand. Another creature caught my attention, causing me to jump backward. Now I faced a six-legged creature, about half my size, that looked something like a cross between a sloth and a very large house cat, with gray and brown-mottled fur, triangular ears sitting on the top of its head, and long, sharp claws. It uttered something incomprehensible, and it raised up on its hind four limbs and grabbed me with the other two.

My stomach flip-flopped, and a sense of paralysis overcame me. I couldn't even catch my breath to scream as the spider approached and placed something over my head.

I closed my eyes as knowledge flooded my mind, so fast I thought my brain was cooking. Sounds broke through the commotion and became voices I could understand.

The sloth-like creature spoke. "Don't give it too much. We don't know if it's even intelligent."

Horse-sized spider replied. "I'm just giving it the male grinkun education level. Enough so it can stay out of the way of the caravan bots. If it can't handle that, we'll send it to protein recovery."

"Ginnamorana M'Duhra would be upset if this thing went there. It's her pet. She made me promise to check on it and bring it back, alive even. Of course, if it can't handle the training, that's not my fault, and she'd have to get over it."

The spider raised a pair of arms as if in a defensive pose. "I don't want to get on her bad side. She's got a reputation."

"I'm not afraid of her."

"Well, I can't phase shift as you can. If she decided I was to be her dinner, there's little I could do to fend her off."

"You don't have enough meat on you for her to bother. Look, I think it's coming around." The sloth-cat poked me in the chest. "Can you understand me?"

"Yes."

"Good. I'm Solondrex Bavindro Kallu." He rolled his hand ever so slowly as he talked. "Kallu is a title of honor; it means I'm fully advanced."

"Solond... Slowhand," I said.

"By the gods, it's stupid," Slowhand said as he began to walk away. "Follow me."

"What about my clothes? I had some gear..."

"It's all on Sarge."

"Can I get something to cover up with?"

The spider seemed to nod in understanding. He opened a white, octagonal crate with nimble spider fingers and retrieved a wide strip of fabric larger than a bath towel and handed it to me.

"Thank you."

"I'll add it to the tab."

Slowhand watched me tie the fabric around my waist and then said, "Try to keep up."

That wasn't difficult. He moved at a pace that would bore a turtle. A small creature, looking a lot like a dirt covered, bipedal possum, approach. *Grinkun,* I thought. *But how did I know that?* My mind went back to the spider, and the name arenea came to mind. And when I thought of the huge one laying eggs, the simple name of Mother Spider entered my mind.

Slowhand must have noticed I was deep in thought. "You look like your head is about to explode. If it does, try to direct it away from me."

I blinked several times before asking, "Are you with Ginn?"

"No, I'm with you. Ginn's back on Sarge. Are you really that dense?"

"I didn't mean right now. I meant, are you two friends?"

"Friends? I don't have friends. If my goals align with another creature's goals, I'll work with them. Ginnamorana fits into that group. She and I have the same common motivation."

"If you and she aren't friends, why are you here?"

Slowhand's eyes squinted and his ears perked up. "She promised me a reward for doing her babysitting. That's all."

"Can I bother you to tell me what that reward might be?"

Slowhand's eyes lit up. "Trilatinum ingots, or more commonly, electronic credits or tokens that represent those ingots. Nobody wants to carry around hundreds of pounds of actual trilatinum."

"I see. Can you tell me what has happened? Where am I?"

"A lot has happened, and I don't have the time or patience to tell you everything since the Colossal Crack. You're going to have to narrow it down, drastically."

"Can you start with why I was in that egg-thing?"

"That egg was the only thing with the ability to save your life. You wouldn't be here now if it weren't for that egg."

"I suppose I owe that giant Mother Spider a thank you."

Slowhand's lip curled into a snarl. "Why would you thank the Mother Spider? She's not cognizant."

"If she's not aware, how did I get into the egg? You didn't feed me to her, did you?"

"I don't know the specifics of how biology works for your species, but I can assure you, getting you into that egg required an approach nowhere near the Mother Spider's mouth. It was the opposite end."

My jaw dropped. "Are you saying you put me in her…"

"Now you're getting it." Slowhand smiled a toothy grin.

"And she allowed this?"

"She had no idea. It was the arenea who allowed us to insert you into an unfertilized royal egg. At the cost of quite a few credits, I might add."

"You paid that spider guy to get me into that egg? Why?"

"I didn't pay anything. Why would I? I have no concern if you live or die. Ginnamorana entered a contract with the arenea for that service."

"Why would she do that?"

"Even if I knew, I'm sure I wouldn't understand." He pointed toward an opening in the hallway with several signs on it. "I need to drop some kids off at the pool. Are you good?"

"What?"

"Lay pipe, feed the recycler, go doody? Do any of those terms mean anything to you?"

The signs began making sense in my mind. This was the bathroom, but there were so many options. "Now I understand. But I'm not sure which way to go."

"Well, considering I saw you standing there naked, I can assume you could use one of these two." He nodded toward a couple of signs; they looked like squiggles of nonsense. "Do you require vacuum assistance?"

"What? No!" I said.

"Then don't go into that one." He twisted his ears toward his right. "Try this one. It's fairly universal."

The facility was fitted with an opening close enough to a latrine that I was able to utilize it without hurting myself, so I considered that a minor victory. I returned to the hall and waited for Slowhand while watching a red, bat-like creature flutter past me and enter the bathroom. Would it hang upside down while relieving itself? That position wouldn't be practical unless its plumbing was completely different than any critter I'd ever seen.

Slowhand emerged and walked a little faster now. "I need to tell you about Sarge. He has some serious memory issues, so until we can get you installed into his permanent banks, he may think you are hostile. If this happens, just tell him you are Private... What is your name, anyway?"

"Idiom Lee."

"Private Idiom Lee. Tell him you're a new recruit, and you joined to kill some damned crystals. He gets off on that kind of talk."

"Crystals?"

"Just play along with him. He'll forget what you say within a few minutes, anyway." We walked down a long hall that ended with a thick, metal door equipped with a long handle. "Before you open this door, make certain you don't see a red light glowing above it. Red means dead; get it?"

"I can remember that."

Slowhand raised up and grasped the handle with four hands, pulling it downward. The door opened by sliding back away from us and then toward the side. "This is our docking bay, number B163. And this," he said gesturing to the left, "is Sarge."

Something large like a barn stood before me, but somehow it looked as if it could move. It was angular in design, like a rail car or large stagecoach, and it was multicolored as if sections of it had come from different sources. The side facing me was red on the left, and yellow on the right, with the letters "AMBUL" in one script, and "XI" in another. It had one angled glass lantern on one side, the other was round, giving it the look of a surly sailor. A loading ramp extended on one side, right where the color changed from red to blue.

"What is this thing?" I asked.

"This thing is Sarge. He's a combination of several decommissioned vessels. Part police cruiser, ambulance, taxi, and private vehicle, he's one of a kind in this universe, and he's here because of me."

I ran my hand across the exterior of Sarge, trying to find a seam where the pieces had been forged together, but it was as smooth as a single pane of glass. If it weren't for the color shift or variations in design, you'd never know they'd once been separate pieces. "How did you weld this together?"

"Normally, a question like that would be an insult, but I'll give you a pass this one time. I did not weld this ship together; I phased it together."

"Phased?"

"I doubt you'll understand it, but I'll try to dumb it down for you. Imagine you are looking at an extremely fine needle laying on a flat surface. Now if I turn that needle so it is perfectly facing one eye, and you closed the other one, you couldn't see it. It's still there, but it's disappeared. When I phase shift, I can turn matter to the perpendicular dimension, so it disappears. Then I can pull the pieces together and phase them back to the normal orientation. That creates a perfect seam that happens to be stronger than the surrounding material, twice as strong in fact. By itself, it's quite a special ship. But we've added one more thing that no other ship like it has. Allow me to introduce you to Sarge." Slowhand motioned for me to climb the ramp inside.

I found the floor to be cold and rough on my bare feet, and my nose caught a whiff of air that reminded me of the smell after a thunderstorm. I grabbed a handhold, and as I entered I noticed the walls were covered in window panes filled with images, charts and words. I touched the picture of a bell-shaped object to learn the glass was rubbery and bent beneath my finger. The image blurred until I pulled my my hand back. *They've got some fancy pictures here.*

"Intruder alert!" The voice boomed from above. I looked around but saw nothing but an empty vessel. "Security squadron Delta Seven, report immediately to the loading ramp! Security, why aren't you responding?"

"It's because we don't have a security force, Sarge," Slowhand said.

"Well, paint me pink and call me a petunia. What's happened to our security force?" Sarge asked.

Slowhand made a silly face, drooping his tongue out over his lip. "Don't worry about it. This guy is with me."

"What is your designation, son?" Sarge asked.

Out of habit, I began to tip my hat before realizing it was gone. "Private Lee."

"Privately? You can speak freely here, no reason to worry about this fellow just because he's grown a couple of extra limbs. It throws me off as well sometimes, but he's cleared security."

"Private Idiom Lee. I, uh, just wanted to break some glass."

Slowhand stared at me as if he were about to smack me. "He's a joker, Sarge. He means he wants to kill some crystals. Don't you, Private?"

That's right, Slowhand had said crystals. "Umm, yes, I hate those damn crystals! I want to kill every single one of them!"

"Oo-Rah! Now that's what I like to hear!" Sarge said. "Why are you out of uniform, soldier?"

Slowhand sighed. "Sarge, he got a little too excited on shore leave. That's why I had to go get him."

"Ah, yes, shore leave. You should see the Medical Sergeant. Don't want to get any invaders in your privates, Private!"

Slowhand laughed. "Thanks for that, Sarge. Have you seen Ginnamorana?"

"She left at oh-seven-thirty. Said she needed to meet with a contact regarding a job."

I looked around to see if I could find Sarge. *Perhaps he was simply around a corner or in another room?*

"Did you need something?" Slowhand asked.

"I would like to find my clothes and kit."

He pointed to a small door. "It's in this locker. I'll wait outside. I've already seen enough of you." Slowhand said. "Don't be messing around in there while I'm gone."

I was relieved to find my clothes had been stored there, and it appeared they had also been cleaned. I poked a finger through a bullet hole in my pants and put them on. The strange thing was, there wasn't a matching scar on my leg. *That egg must have been some medicine.* I stuck my finger through a hole in my duster and shirt as well, but no indication of an injury. After getting completely dressed and reloading my pistols, I put my hat on, even though I was inside. I just feel naked without my hat.

What have I gotten myself into? Nothing good ever comes from getting involved, yet, like a big idiot I had to get myself caught up in some crazy crap. A smart man would have ignored the scream and simply rode on to the Rusty Anvil. I could have stayed one night and left before Clyde and Darrel showed up. If they hadn't found me there, they might have given up and gone back home. They'd still be alive and I'd not be stuck here.

I stepped out to find Slowhand yawning widely. "Can I ask you about Sarge? I didn't see anybody. It was like I was talking to the air. Was he phasing?"

"Of course not! Sarge can't phase, that's something only I can do. Sarge is an A.I."

"A.I.? Is that some kind of sailor talk?"

"It stands for Artificial Intelligence."

I ran a finger and thumb across the brim of my hat in thought, trying to guess what that could be. "And that means?"

"Which word are you having trouble with?"

"I know what each one means, but I've never heard them used together as if they have some special meaning. Where is Sarge?"

"He is a construct within electronic systems. Think of him as a brain, and the ship is his body."

"Is he alive?"

Slowhand's face contorted as if he were in pain talking to me. "He's not biological if that's what you mean. But he is intelligent, and his capabilities allow us to do things others in our position cannot."

"What kind of things?"

"This ship shouldn't be able to create Null Space Conduits. But with Sarge onboard, we can."

My head started to ache like I was trying to learn new math. "Null Space?"

"Don't worry about it. It just means we can go farther and faster than the other contractors out here."

"You're a contractor?"

"Well, we aren't military."

"I've got a lot to learn."

"That you do, and I tire of this conversation as I'm late for a nap. Why don't you wait for Ginnamorana to return, perhaps over there where you can't get into trouble?" He pointed toward a corner of the bay where some crates were propped up against one another.

"Got it. I'll wait." I sat on one of the cold, hard and extremely uncomfortable crates. Curiosity got the better of me, so I tried to open it. I ran my hands over the corners, top, and front, searching for a latch or mechanism.

Ginn entered the bay, and said, "Careful with that. It's filled with fuel pellets."

"Ginn! I'm glad to see you. Glad to see you in this form especially." My face flushed red and grew warm.

She approached slowly, her eyes scanning me head to toe as if searching for something gone wrong. "It appears the arenea fulfilled their end of the bargain. Have you noticed any side effects?

"What should I be looking for?"

"Sprouting compound eyes or extra limbs, or perhaps producing silk from a gland on your back?"

My pulse raced. "Not that I've noticed."

She silently walked around me as if looking for any extra bits growing from me. "That's good. Of course, if the egg hadn't been unfertilized, the arenea would have shredded you on the spot, so you're probably good." She led the way, walking a wide circle around Sarge.

Not know what else to do, I followed her. "I'll admit I'm having a hard time processing all of this."

"I suppose this would be quite a shock for you. Here's the short version. You're no longer on Earth."

"Is this some kind of a joke? Tell me exactly where I am?"

"Docking bay B163."

I gave her a side-eye glance. "That tells me nothing."

"We are currently inside a habitable asteroid called Panadaras. It's traveling between galactic systems."

A sense of dread overcame me. "What in blazes are you saying?"

"We're in space, Idiom. A long way from Earth. While you were recovering in that egg, this asteroid has made what's called a VLR Null Space jump."

"What does that even mean?"

"The VLR stands for Very Long Range."

I found myself breathing faster than I should have been. "Slowhand mentioned Null Space Condolences earlier."

"Slowhand? Condolences?"

"The fuzzy fellow with two extra arms. Looks like a surly cat mated with a sloth."

Ginn sighed. "Solondrex, and I'm certain he said conduits."

I leaned against the wall as my head spun. "So what does this mean?"

"It's all very complicated, Idiom. Let's start with the important stuff. You're alive, and we now owe the arenea twenty thousand trilatinum credits. We're too far away from the next system to try to earn those credits planetside, so we need to earn them here. I have a job I need you to do, and if you succeed, we'll pay off your debt."

"Can you at least explain how you turned into that thing?"

"I don't want to discuss that now. Once you've done this job and we're clear, I might tell you more, if I so choose."

"It sounds like I don't have much choice in the matter."

"None."

CHAPTER FIVE
SHADOW HUNTING

"Let me get this straight." I leaned forward and rested my forehead in my hand. "Somewhere on this planet…"

"Asteroid. Panadaras is a heavy metal asteroid, hollowed out and converted into a ship," Ginn said, correcting me.

"Got it. Somewhere on this asteroid, there is a shadow thing."

"A shade. Are you even paying attention? He's a shade. You'll recognize him because he looks like he's always in the shadow, even in the brightest light. As you approach him, you'll notice the air surrounding him is colder than normal."

"Like a ghost?"

"No, for the umpteenth time, he's a shade. You'll have a hard time focusing on him, because of the time fluctuations."

I shook my head. "Time fluctuations?"

"Shades have limited control of time surrounding them. If attacked, they can move faster than you can see. They also are rumored to be able to stop a person's heart or other important organs upon touch."

"Right. When I see a strange shadow, you want me to strap on a temporary dil..."

Ginn's eyebrows raised in anger. "Temporal diode." She produced a metallic sleeve from a drawer. "This goes on your forearm. The clamps will self-adjust."

"Fine, then when I have this guy in my sites, I need to grab him while wearing that thing. Then some bushwhackers swoop in to capture him and drag him off."

Ginn's face contorted as if she was getting frustrated with this conversation. "What you call bushwhackers are migrun security officers, but that's the general idea. The diode will alert them upon initiation with your location, so all you need to do is hold on. The migrun are willing to pay off the arenea and cover several cycles of rent."

"I see. So, what did this guy do? Why's he wanted?"

"He's a shade, Idiom. These things aren't natural."

"You turn into some mutant bear thing and Slowhand has six limbs, but a shade isn't natural? Can you tell me he killed somebody, stole their beans, or ate their cat or something?"

"Idiom, when you encounter the shade, you'll get a glimpse of your fate, and it's always a horribly painful experience."

"Why do the migraines want him?"

Ginn raised her arms as she talked. "They're called migruns and how would I know? To scare their kids? I don't know, and truthfully, I don't care."

"Do you trust them?"

"Nobody trusts the migruns."

"Yet we're capturing and handing over a spook to them."

"A shade."

"Whatever. Do you have a clue where I can find him? Point me in the right direction at least?"

Ginn pressed a button on the table, and a three-dimensional image appeared out of thin air. "This is Panadaras."

"Looks like a rock with fire shooting out its backside."

"That's actually a decent description of it. The top seven levels are all migrun military controlled. Completely off-limits to us as well as the shade. The bottom four levels are called common areas."

"That doesn't even cover the top half of this rock. What's below the lowest level?"

"Grinkun mines, for the most part," Ginn said.

Slowhand entered yawning, his fur unkept as if he'd just woken. He raised two of his arms, pointing at the very bottom of the image of the rock. "If we're going into that level of detail, we might as well tell him about the micro layer of element zero on the bottom. That's what gives us the sense of gravity."

"Sense of gravity?" I asked.

Ginn shrugged. "Didn't the arenea give you the basics? This is all kid-level knowledge. Element zero, when properly charged creates a graviton field equal to its own mass times ten to the twenty-fourth power." She seemed to pinch the air in front of her, and the image changed to show an interior layout. "Now we've gotten past first-grade physics; we are here." She pointed.

"Docking bay B163."

"Right."

"I'm assuming there are saloons on this rock?"

"Of course," Ginn replied.

"And the darkest, seediest one is where?"

"Bottom level, furthest back toward the engines. Few go in there but grinkun and fools."

"Then I should be welcome there." I studied the layout long enough to get my bearings, grabbed the temporal thing, and started walking.

I passed creatures my mind couldn't comprehend. Something fluttered by me on gossamer wings as transparent as glass with a ball-shaped body without eyes or face. Once it passed, the air smelled like someone was cooking a latrine's contents over an open fire. A metallic creature rolled along the floor, three wheels on each side formed a triangle. When it came to a threshold, the entire triangle rotated instead of just the bottom two wheels. Another creature scurried upside down along the ceiling. None of them seemed threatening, and each seemed to have their own agenda.

Two ramps led me to the lowest common level, and after a few minutes, I found the entrance to a large room filled with all manner of creatures, the rumble of dozens of voices, and some form of music filled the air. This must be the saloon.

I cased the room, looking for any weird shadow thing I could find, passing what looked like a mass of brown, writhing insects. As I stared at it they wiggled together to form the shape of a human. I realized they were copying my form when their movements matched my own. *That may cause me nightmares.*

I tried to act like I was comfortable here, while surrounded by unimaginable aliens of all forms, shapes, and colors. I watched a pair of glowing slugs move toward one another and merge as one, and as they did, their light changed from yellow to green.

"What'll you have?" a green-skinned, frog-mouthed creature asked from behind a counter as soon as I entered.

"Uh, I'm a little short on trilaxitive credits."

"No trilatinum? Surely you have something of value," Froggy croaked.

I fished through my pockets. "I have some silver dollars."

"Let me see those." He reached out and snagged one of the coins. "I've never seen one of those before, and rare means valuable. I'll give you a drink for this one."

"Thank you. What do you have?"

"Hundreds of options. What does your species require to obtain an intoxicating effect?"

My eyes took in dozens of spigots coming out of rectangular containers. "Alcohol, whiskey if you've got it."

"We have muldarian milk. Careful, it's flammable."

"Is it safe? I won't go blind from drinking it, will I?"

The barkeep winked one eye toward me. "It's all natural and marked safe for ninety-nine percent of known species,"

"That'll work." Froggy kept the dollar, tossing it into a chest that opened after he squinted at it. When the lid popped open, a variety of coin, paper, and gems shined under the lights. A moment later he brought me a warm glass of some thick liquid.

"Here's mud in your eye," I said, taking a drink. It was bitter and a thick, but I'd had rotgut just as bad. It reminded me of the time my friend Jack had borrowed his dad's "medicine" and we drank it in the barn loft. My stomach churned at the memory of throwing up all over a pile of hay.

Froggy wiped both eyes with his hand before walking away. I sipped my drink, welcoming the warmth and calming effect of the alcohol.

I caught a glimpse of a shadow in a corner. I steeled my nerves and made my approach, acting as if the table were empty. I found a stool suitable for me to sit on, looking away from the shadow the entire time. The hairs on my arms stood erect as a cold chill overtook me. The darkness was hard to focus on. I'd get a glimpse of a thin, harrowed face for a moment, to see it hold still and then it would move quickly and disappear, only to repeat the process again and again. What looked like clouds of black vapor emanated from its body, while skeletal hands silently tapped the table. My heart raced in anticipation. Perhaps it was the alcohol, but sitting next to what I would have called Death himself a day ago, I just felt a sense of wonder, not terror. I had to say something.

"Oh, hi. I thought this table was empty."

"You are most unusual. Most beings have the good sense to flee when they encounter me," the shade said, his voice distorting. He pointed toward me with a long bony finger. "What do you want?" His face contorted to show pointed, long teeth.

This guy is bluffing. I shrugged, smiling a bit. "Want? That's a good question. All this is new to me. I suppose all I can ask for is a safe place to enjoy my drink."

"I sense no fear in you. Are you capable of fearing death itself?" His eyes seemed to glow like tiny candles in the distance on a clouded, moonless night.

"I'm Idiom Lee," I said. *Is this my chance? Should I turn on this temporal thing and grab his hand?* I decided not to, at least not yet.

"Rhuldan Krahl."

"Nice to meet you, Rodan Crawl."

He seemed to laugh. his thin lips turned upward. "Are you aware that with the touch of my finger, I can end your life, Idiom Lee?"

"Listen, in the last few days, I've seen enough stuff to keep me from sleeping for the next thirty years. You're no scarier to me than watching a woman turn into a creepy bear or a sixty-foot spider's ass a couple feet from my head. Nothing personal, but my senses are probably burned to ash. That death-touch thing sounds handy, though."

"Death-touch? I like that term. Mind if I use it?"

"Be my guest." Movement in the corner of my eye caught my attention. I watched without turning my head to see a creature. It had a roughly human shape with a pale-beige face, bright orange eyes, and curled pointed ears covered in multi-hued feathers, It wore a dark blue military-style uniform. I glanced the opposite way to see another approaching. This one's eyes were green, but clearly they were the same species. *The Bushwhackers are here. But I haven't activated this temporal diode thing.*

The shade's eyes dimmed into nothing. "We approach a critical juncture. Which side will you stand with?"

"Tell me, what are you guilty of?"

"Only the crime of protecting myself when attacked without hesitation. None have survived such an encounter."

His mouth looked threatening, but his eyes looked almost pleading.

"Nothing more?"

"Nothing worth speaking of."

I looked downward. "I've done the same and would do it again."

"Then we're a lot alike. Do you believe in due process?"

I squinted at him. *Does he know I trained as a lawyer?* "Where I come from, we have an idea of innocent until proven guilty. Will the migrun give you a fair trial?"

"If they apprehend me, they'll either kill me immediately, or worse. I expect they want to harvest my temporal power."

I sensed honesty in his words, and I didn't like the idea of these birdmen jumping the gun. "How do we play this?"

"The migrun will charge. I sense their temporal diodes restricting time around them. If they grab me, I'll be stuck in chronological synchronicity. If that happens, I'll be caught."

"Any idea why they want you?"

"They want what I can do."

"And that is?"

"My best guess is to offer a complete and impenetrable defense for their leader. They will charge in five seconds. Decide now."

The migrun on my left lunged toward Rhuldan. I leaped up and threw a punch at his feathered, beaked face, and I heard a sickening sound of breaking bone. The other migrun grabbed Rhuldan's arm and shook the shade. Peeking out from beneath the bushwhacker's sleeve, I could see the temporal doohickey on his arm. Without thinking, I drew one of my Colts and aimed at the device. I squeezed the trigger, releasing a deafening clap of thunder and hot lead. Sparks flew, and Rhuldan returned to his normal, shadowy self.

"Now to end this." Rhuldan raised a bony finger toward the nearest migrun, whose eyes opened in terror.

I yelled, "Stop! It doesn't have to end in death."

Rhuldan's face quivered as if behind dark clouds, but his expression showed surprise. "Why should I spare them?"

"You kill them, and next time they'll send twenty instead of two. Let them live, and they'll fear you forever. Trust me on this."

Rhuldan grumbled and sighed. "Fine, we'll try it your way. Now let's get out of here before more come." He grabbed my arm, and I wondered if he'd kill me, but my heart kept ticking. I did my best to keep up, as I had a strange sense of fighting against the normal order of things as I moved. I relived the same moment several times over before dashing forward. He led me to a closet in the back of the saloon, the floor covered by a heavy crate. Rhuldan opened the lid. A false floor opening led to a ladder. Down was the only way we could go.

The ladder ended at a rocky floor where feet, smaller than mine, had worn away at the path. "What's your plan?" I asked as I followed a dark shadow through a poorly lit tunnel.

"Plan? What makes you think I have a plan?"

"Hope springs eternal? Does this happen to you a lot?" I asked, catching my breath.

"Most life forms either ignore me or make it a point to stay away from me. Only a few are willing to approach, and when they do, I sense an imminent attack, so I dispose of them without delay or remorse. If the migrun didn't have the temporal diodes, I'd be all but impervious to their attempts. Pity you had to destroy that one with your primitive projectile weapon. If I could study one, I might be able to create a counter-measure."

"Then you're in luck." I showed him the device Ginn had given me.

"You had this all along? I have ample reason to finish you!"

"Wait! Let me explain! You see, I owe the spiders a lot of trilaxitive, and my friends, if you can call them that, told me this was the only way to settle the score. But I wanted to hear you out and get a sense of what was right before using this thing. That's why I didn't use it."

Rhuldan stopped and stared at me. His face contorted with as if he were moving quickly then stopping dead, and his mouth's movements didn't seem to match the sound of his words. "Are you certain the migruns just didn't preempt your action?"

"Yes. I was told I'd get a sense of impending doom when I neared you, but I never felt that way. More a sense of wonder and trust."

"Strange. I had a similar experience. Pity I have no choice but to kill you now."

I jumped back, resting my hand on my pistols. "Now hold on a second! I thought we were in this together!"

"That was what I understand is a joke. Your face! It went a new shade of white!" His mouth opened widely, either an indication of laugher or he was about to bite my arm off.

"Very funny, picking on the cowboy from Earth." I held out the temporal diode to him and said, "Here, you want this thing?"

Rhuldan stopped in a dark shadow beneath a metal support beam that curved to the ground. In this light I was afraid to look away from him as he might just disappear. "Keep it for now. When we get to a place I can analyze it, I will. But for now, it is better if you carry it. If it were to discharge on my arm, who knows what it might do to me?"

"You think it's safe for me?"

He shrugged. "That depends. Does your species require fluctuations in the flow of time to circulate blood, or do you possess hearts?"

"Heart. Just one."

"Then you should be fine." Rhuldan raised a single finger toward his face and whispered, "I hear something."

Small footsteps sounded in the distance. I found a crevice big enough for us to duck into, hoping whatever approached us would continue on past. I wasn't so lucky. A grinkun, hunched over and covered in dirt stopped, looked at us, and said, "Outsiders! Not supposed to be here!" He ran away before we could respond.

"We need to stop him!" I ran after the possum-fellow. Rhudlan zipped past me without making a noise. "If I were him, I'd be grabbing my friends, or some guards."

"Do you want me to kill him?" Rhuldan asked. His voice sounded too casual about it, like he didn't care either way.

"No. Just stop him. Keep him quiet too!" My boots slid as I rounded a corner to find our little rat-nosed friend stopped, looking back at us.

"Hey there, buddy," I said, holding my hands away from my pistols. "We're not going to hurt you. We're just hiding for a little while."

Rhuldan raised a finger toward the grinkun.

"Don't! No death-touch!"

"We may not have a choice. I hear more of them coming. Your weapons should be powerful enough to kill them. Are you willing to let them capture you?"

I steeled my nerves. "Let's not do any killing today. I'll talk to them and explain that we're just hiding out for a little while and mean them no harm. I have a good feeling about this!"

CHAPTER SIX
INTO THE FIRE

"Rhuldan, can you hear me?" I tried to say into the darkness, but the gag in my mouth silenced any attempt at talking. Tiny hands had tied my arms and legs together using strong ropes and multiple layers of knots. Behind me, somewhere, those ropes connected to a series of pulleys. I knew this because the grinkun had used them to raise me ten feet above the ground.

Movement in the rope and a slight noise from above me indicated something had returned to us. I craned my neck upward toward the sound, but the room was so dark I couldn't see anything but shadows playing against a black backdrop. Something hairy brushed against my face, and my body convulsed as if ten thousand spiders had walked across my cheek. The gag loosened in my mouth and dropped to my neck.

"Gah! That thing tastes like the south end of a northbound buffalo!"

"What is buffalo?" a high-pitched voice trilled.

"Big, hairy, stinky, stupid animal," I said. "Who's there? I can't see you."

"Are you blind?"

"I certainly hope not. I see a little light here and there."

A voice from below me said, "He's a topsider. His eyes are weak."

"Light a torch," the voice from above replied. A spark below me grew into a flame. As the fire lit the room, I became able to see the possum-like, nasty smile of a grinkun hanging upside down, gripping the rope above me, holding a sharp knife in his teeth. Below me, another carried the burning torch close enough its heat made me squirm. Five others circled me, pointing spears in my direction.

"That's better. Now, can we talk?" I asked.

"We are talking."

"That's true. Can you let me down?"

"Of course we can."

"Great, just do it slowly."

"Just because we can do something doesn't mean we will." Several grinkuns from below laughed a high-pitched staccato.

Great. Either grinkuns are smart alecks or literalists. Either way, I need to be careful. "I mean you no harm."

"We've been told those words repeatedly from topsiders, just before they round us up and force us to do their bidding. Why should we trust you any more than the migrun?"

"Listen, I don't have any love for the migrun. That's who we were trying to hide from when we came here."

"It's true," Rhuldan said from across the room. I couldn't find him in the limited light, but based upon his voice, he was facing me, perhaps thirty feet away. "You should have seen what he did to the last migrun who crossed his path. That bird will be spending the next few weeks regrowing cheekbones!"

The grinkun pursed his lips and shook his head. "Why should I believe you? I think you work for the nasty birds."

Rhuldan said, "The migrun tried to capture me. If it hadn't been for Idiom, they'd have me."

"Idiom? What is Idiom?" Upside down grinkun asked.

"I am Idiom."

"What should we do?" one of the grinkuns below me asked.

"Kill him. I don't trust him," another.

"No! We'll ask the commander. He'll decide."

"Yes, he'll know what to do," the grinkun above me said as he scurried away.

"Wait! Let me down before you go!" I said.

"No."

I sighed. Hanging by these ropes was beginning to make it hard to breathe. "Rhuldan, what do you remember? How did they capture us so easily?"

"I remember hearing something coming from the distance. Then we were surrounded on all sides, above and below at once. You said I shouldn't kill them. They covered us in an instant as if it were raining grinkun. That was right after you said you had a good feeling about this."

"Next time I say that, tell me to stop wagging my tongue."

"Without hesitation."

"What do you know about the grinkun?"

"I haven't studied them, but I know they are known for their mining skills. Even without power tools, they can excavate more efficiently than the best automatons. Rumor has it they can see in near-complete darkness, and based upon what we just heard, that rumor is likely true. The males aren't considered intelligent, but there are stories of the females being strong strategists."

"The females are smart, eh? Would they have a queen?"

"More likely a brood mother. She would be their highest ranking official."

"Is she truly their mother? Are they all brothers?"

"I haven't had the opportunity to learn about their reproductive customs, and I wasn't planning on doing any experimentation today. I'd recommend treating their brood mother as if she were royalty. Do you hear that? I think they are returning."

This time the footsteps seemed more patterned as if they were walking in formation. Three lines of grinkun entered, each row was seven deep, and these grinkun wore a bright yellow armor and carried bladed staffs. *Royal guards perhaps?*

"Cut them down." The order came from a fat, white haired grinkun who followed the battalion. He appeared older than the rest and wore a bright red cap that told me he was a commander or leader. A small, fast grinkun ran toward the ropes and began to saw away at them with his blade.

"Wait!" I said, "Can you lower me..." The rope gave way, and I fell flat, belly down, knocking the wind out of me. I coughed and gagged before whimpering out, "...first." Then they cut Rhuldan's rope. He fell faster than I expected, but just before he hit the ground, he came to a near stop, landing without making a sound. *Lucky bastard.*

Commander Fat-Possum waddled around the formation and studied me. "What is this creature?"

A dirt covered grinkun stepped forward. "We don't know. It's a topsider, but the dark one said it struck a migrun."

I wiggled against my ropes, loosening them a bit. "That I did. Punched him square in the face."

When the commander laughed, his jowls wiggled. "What I wouldn't give to see that." He turned back to his soldiers. "Take them to the royal chamber. Don't harm them unless they try to escape."

"What if they try to run?" one soldier asked.

"Kill them, of course."

The winding passageway was too dark for my eyes, and, since the average grinkun was a foot shorter than me, I learned quickly of the need to duck to avoid the low ceiling, and that grinkuns find a topsider smacking his head on a low beam to be hilarious. We took multiple turns before the path opened into a large chamber which was, thankfully, well lit with burning oil lamps. A fat female grinkun leaned against a throne covered in gold and purple regalia. Attendants fed her red berries, while an old grinkun wearing a visor stood beside her. The room fell silent except for the sound of the large female eating.

The Brood Mother twitched her nose as they shoved Rhuldan and me before her, but she didn't bother looking up from her meal. "What are you?"

"Me or him?" I asked.

She chugged a goblet of blue liquid, spilling some down her chin. "You. I'm familiar with shades."

"I'm a human. My name is Idiom Lee."

Old, visor-wearing grinkun's face started to glow in letters I couldn't make out. She made a few grunts as information flashed in her eyes. "Human, regardless of spelling or dialect, does not exist."

I nodded. "Well, that's news to me."

A guard poked me in the back with the butt of his spear. "Show respect or next time I use pointed end."

I nodded toward her. "I meant no disrespect, your majesty. I just got here. All of this is new to me."

The Brood Mother chewed a berry, spitting the pit on the floor for an attendant to grab immediately. "I've been told you struck a migrun. Is this true?"

"Yes. They charged us."

"You have no allegiance to the migrun?"

"Ma'am, in all my life I've met a grand total of two of those bird-looking fellows. One I punched in the face, the other one, let's just say his arm is smarting about now."

"As for you, shade, what is your relationship with the migrun?"

"They tried to capture me without reason. I assume they wanted to kill me or use my powers."

The Brood Mother raised her nose up and sniffed the air twice. "The grinkun need strong warriors to defend ourselves. I'll give you an opportunity to prove your mettle."

A murmur began behind me. Grinkun guards whispered to one another while someone approached. The battalion separated in the middle to allow passage.

A young female grinkun wearing the fanciest pink and white sparkling dress I'd ever seen had entered and it was clear she was important by the way she walked and how the others backed away from her. Bright-white fur flowed behind her and deep blue eyes, the color of a Montana sky glowed. She had an oddly pleasant look to her face — it was cute, more like a dog's face than nasty like a possum. She ran a manicured paw down my arm. "What an interesting specimen we have here."

I had the most unexplainable reaction to the touch, almost an attraction, but more like when you look at a cute puppy and you want to pick it up and cuddle it, but then you realize it's a wolf pup and it may just eat your face off. I snapped out of my odd stupor and said, "Pleasure to meet you, miss."

The Brood Mother spat a half-chewed berry on the floor. "It's so nice of you to join us, my daughter. To what do we owe this visit?"

"I saw the migrun newsfeed. These two have created quite a commotion," the young female said.

"So you wanted to see them for yourself, Fayye?"

"Yes. I need to know if they would be suitable."

The Brood Mother pushed the berry plate away. "Suitable for what, Princess?"

"A special job, dear Mother. Suffice it to say it's a critical matter of grinkun security, and the less we speak of it, the better off we all are."

The Brood Mother's eyes squinted as if she were crushing a bug, and her lips hardly moved as she spoke. "You heard the princess. These two are her property. None are to interfere with her project." She pointed a red, berry-stained hand at her daughter. "Don't make things worse."

"I'd sooner die, Mother." Fayye stared at Rhuldan and me. "This way." We followed her to a room with backlit opalescent walls draped by tapestries featuring all the colors of the rainbow. Several chairs surrounded a table made of polished black stone. Fayye stopped at the door, and without saying a word, she pointed toward the chairs. We sat as she closed the door behind her and pulled the handle tight. She pulled a device smaller than a pistol and mostly flat from her pocket and looked at it as she walked the perimeter of the room.

I started to say something, but before I did, Rhuldan waved at me and raised a single finger toward his mouth.

Fayye pocketed her device. "I had to make sure there weren't any bugs. We can talk freely now."

I leaned my head to the side. "I don't like bugs. My horse Leroy used to draw nasty, big flies. Stung like fire when they bit."

Fayye's lips tightened. She glanced at Rhuldan. "He's not from around here, is he?"

Rhuldan smiled a toothy grin. "No, he's not."

Fayye's gaze went from Rhuldan's feet to his face and then back to his chest. "My apologies, Shade, but I must insist." She opened a tall cabinet and retrieved a long black cape and the finest hat I'd ever seen. Krenshaw would have paid a hundred dollars for that hat, and it might have even made him look good. "Put these on. I find it disturbing to watch you constantly fade in and out like clouds of black smoke."

"Klektian silk," Rhuldan said, taking the garments. "This much is worth a lot of trilatinum. I will accept your gifts." He put them and became a lot easier to focus on, as only his hands and face were now ethereal.

"That's a fine-looking hat. You wouldn't happen to have another, would you, ma'am?"

"Sorry. If I come across another, I'll keep you in mind," Fayye said. "Now allow me to explain a few things. The arenea probably don't care what we do in our war room unless it meant hurting their profits. The migrun, though, would love to know what goes on in here."

I imagined horseflies listening in on my conversations with Leroy. I'd probably get sent to an insane asylum if anyone heard me. "You think they might have a deal with some bugs to listen in on you?"

Rhuldan leaned toward me, raising his palms upward. "She's speaking of electronic listening devices. They're often called 'bugs.'"

"Kind of like Bell's telephone."

Rhuldan's face went blank. "I'll take your word for it."

Fayye rubbed her forehead with a paw. "Now we have that settled, allow me to explain why I've brought you here. My people have had something of value stolen from us, and we're going to get it back."

I sighed. "I swear to God if after all this you're planning a train robbery, I'm out of here."

Fayye looked toward the ceiling. "Considering I don't know what a train robbery is, I think you're safe."

Rhuldan leaned back in his chair. "Are you going to tell us what was stolen?"

Fayye nodded. "My cousin-kin have a mine on a small world known as Hylak. They discovered a vein of nearly pure element zero, more than has been discovered in centuries. Somehow, word of their discovery leaked, and within days, a squadron of migrun commandos stormed the base, who killed anyone who got in their way, prior to stealing twelve hundred pounds of the stuff."

I raised a finger. "Element zero? Wait, I've heard of that. Something about it being used to create gravity, right? The old E.Z. trick."

"Correct," she said. "The bottom of this asteroid has a layer the thickness of a single molecule of it. Once charge to the proper level, it creates our gravity, which makes life here feasible."

"How many asteroids like this one would that mother lode cover, spread thin like that?" I asked.

"Thousands, probably tens of thousands." Fayye shook her head. "The migrun won't need that much for another hundred years."

"Yet they stole it," I said. "What else can it be used for?"

Rhuldan's gaze turned upward. "I've never heard of any other uses."

"One thing I've learned is anything good can be used for bad purposes. If they were to connect a big dynamo directly to twelve hundred pounds of element zero, what would happen?" I asked.

Rhuldan sighed. "We haven't used anything similar to a dynamo in centuries."

"It doesn't matter what you call it. Whatever is used to charge the bottom end of this asteroid. Pretend you hooked that up to the entire chunk."

"It's a fusion cell, and it seems they could use it to create a black hole."

"Ah, yes. A black hole," I said. "And that is?"

Rhuldan cracked his knuckles repeatedly. "That would be bad. Very bad."

I studied his face. Waves of shadow formed and faded. I got the nerve and asked, "Are we talking dynamite bad?"

"We're talking wipe out an entire planet or system bad."

"That is bad. How do we stop them?"

Fayye place her hands on her hips and hissed. "If you were listening, you'd know we're planning on taking it back."

"But how?"

"I happen to know the migrun have taken it to a processing facility on Khutanga. That facility will be well shielded and guarded, and only a surgical strike team has a chance of getting in and out alive."

"So where do we fit into all of this?" I asked.

"You two will be a part of that team."

"Us two?" Rhuldan and I spoke at the same time.

"Of course. That's why I saved you from Mother, remember?"

CHAPTER SEVEN
DREAM TEAM

I sat on a hard rock shelf dug out of the wall in a room the Grinkun called guest quarters. A single oil-lamp hung from the ceiling, and a roughly cut door made of a black hardwood hung partially open to allow some air movement. My stomach hurt, I was hot and I felt miserable. Rhuldan knocked on the doorframe of my spartan quarters in the grinkun mine. I glanced up at him from my bunk. "Hi."

"I don't know much about your species, but from what I have learned, you look terrible."

"I feel terrible. I think it's the grinkun food. I eat it, and it spends all of about ten minutes inside me before demanding to escape from one end or another."

"I'd wager it's not the food."

"The water then?"

Rhuldan leaned in to study my face. He got close enough it made me uncomfortable. "When you hatched out of that egg, what was the first thing you noticed?"

"Besides the huge spider's butt above me?"

"Yes."

I thought about it for a moment, reliving the moments right after getting here. "The intensity of all the colors and sounds. Everything seemed to be more vivid."

"The process you went through does more than basic healing. It also strips away anything that isn't you or supposed to be there. Such as the bullets in your body, any cataracts on your eyes, and unfortunately, any helpful biotics in your gut."

"What are you saying? I didn't have any bi-optics in my stomach."

Rhuldan backed away several inches. I was glad he did. "Biotics. In many species, they are tiny microbes that help in the digestion of food. I think you are missing them now."

"I'm missing something. How do we get them back?"

"I'll talk to the grinkun. I think they can help you. Meantime, Fayye wants to see to us. She's ready to introduce us to the team."

"Let me put my boots on, and I'll be right there." I stood up and swayed. Rhuldan grabbed my arm to steady me, and I felt the time waves as if I were standing still and running all at once. The sensation made me even more sick, so I pushed his hand away. "I'm good." I followed him to the war room.

"There you are." Fayye welcomed us. "I'd like to introduce you to the team." She pointed to the polished black table where three strange looking, six-inch-tall creatures stood.

I leaned in toward Rhuldan's ear to whisper, "They're a little small, aren't they?"

"They're holograms, Idiom."

"They're still likely to get stepped on if I need to run to the latrine. Is Fayye serious? This is the best she can find? A fat house cat could make a meal out of these boys."

"They're not physically here. That's just a projection. In reality, they are about the same size as we are."

"Oh. Hollow grands. Never mind."

"Are you two done?" Fayye's eyes seemed to cut us down.

"Yes."

"Good." She made a motion with her paw, and two of the tiny creatures disappeared, while one seemed to grow to twice his size. He looked like an iguana had mated with a knight in armor, wearing shiny metal plates over green-scaled skin. A forked tongue danced between sharp teeth. "Gorthul, please introduce yourself and tell us your specialty."

"I am Gorthul. Captain of the ship, *Onyx Infiltrator*, perhaps you've heard of her?" His mouth opened unnaturally wide, displaying dozens of ivory points as he laughed. "Of course not, because she's never been spotted despite thirty-six successful retrieval missions against tougher bases than this one. My job is to get the team in and out without being detected or shot down. In all the galaxy, there does not exist another ship with the active and passive stealth systems as mine."

"Thank you Gorthul." Fayye waved her paw. Gorthul shrank to nothing.

Another creature appeared. This one had a metallic sheen across his entire body, and a flat, rectangular head with no face, just a line of black circles where I'd expect eyes to be. "My designation is Dreydus Seven Oh Six. I am an unrestricted cipher-droid, with direct quantum connection to *Penseur*."

"Pinch her? I'd advise against that. She's got some powerful guards," I said.

"*Penseur* is the most powerful dark-computer in the galaxy. My job is to hack into any system, door or computer needed. I can crack the toughest migrun passcodes in milliseconds."

"That sounds important," I said, even though I had no clue what any of that meant.

Fayye moved her paw again, this time I saw a six-limbed beast with a face reminding me of a rhinoceros, complete with golden horn. Muscles flexed and bulged as this thing did nothing more than breathe. If I had to guess, he was the enforcer of this operation.

"I am Jekto. I bash heads and haul loot. Mostly, I like bashing heads."

I nodded. "That's what I figured. It sounds like we have a good team here."

"The best trilatinum can buy," Fayye said. She motioned until the iguana-guy reappeared. "Gorthul, how far out are you?"

"We'll be overtaking Panadaras in approximately twenty hours. Our approach will be invisible to the migrun authorities. Can you provide us a docking bay left open?"

"Bay D496 will be waiting for your arrival. We'll meet you there." Fayye ended the connection, and the tiny aliens disappeared into nothing. "Any questions from you two?"

"I have a question," I said. "Why do you need us? These guys seem to have it all figured out. What can we do to help?"

Fayye poured three glasses of something dark, handing one to Rhuldan and me, keeping one for herself. "Have you ever worked with mercenaries, Idiom?"

"Hired guns, yes."

"Did you trust them?"

I crossed my arms. "Not for a moment."

"There you have your answer. These hired guns, as you call them, are loyal up to the point of getting their share of trilatinum. The moment they think they can make an extra credit selling us out to the migrun, they will. I want you two there to keep them honest."

"And how are we supposed to do that?"

Fayye raised her paws to the air like a snake-oil salesman about to tell you the miracles of his elixir. "Idiom Lee, the Migrun Pounder and Rhuldan, the Angel of Death! Your images are all over the dark networks. You two are anti-heroes, and your reputation grows with the day. Did you know one time you punched your way through an entire formation of migrun shock troopers, unarmed and outnumbered thirty to one?"

I shrugged. "I punched one birdman in the face."

"Not according to the legends I'm hearing. And you, Rhuldan! A single touch of your finger can kill a soldier and his entire lineage, as if he never existed."

Rhuldan looked away from Fayye and sipped his drink. "These stories are not true."

"Truth is nothing compared to reputation," Fayye said. "These mercenaries might believe about half the stories they've heard about you two, and that's enough for them to behave as long as you are part of the team."

"So why do you trust us?"

"I know the truth, and if you double-cross me, I'll turn you in to the migrun for the bounty on your heads."

I tried the drink. It tasted like almonds cooked in kerosene, so I assumed it was strong. "Sounds like we don't have any choice in the matter."

"None," Fayye said. "At least not until you've retrieved and returned the element zero to me. Then you'll have lots of options."

I looked at Rhuldan. "Do you have any better ideas?"

"The best I have is to enjoy our drinks. This stuff is pretty good; what's it called?"

"Industrial degreaser," Fayye replied.

Rhuldan brought me some undercooked grinkun bread, explaining their preparation process would likely be able to introduce the needed biotics to my gut. I didn't want to know the details but was willing to try anything to fix my stomach problems. The bread had a damp, yeasty flavor, and I kept it down for almost a half hour. A minor victory. We had some time to kill before the mercenaries would arrive, so I taught him how to play poker. I was glad we weren't playing for money because he learned *way* too quickly. That or he was better at cheating than I was.

After my third meal of grinkun bread, I began to gain strength and was able to keep food in my stomach for a while where it belonged. I explored the area around my room and found a grinkun community going about their daily lives. Young ones played and chased each other with pure joy as a few adults watched over them. I imagined the adults to be grandparents lovingly caring for their kin while their own children worked. A pup rubbed against my leg in a friendly manner. I stroked its fur to the sound of a pleasant, rolling purr. Several others joined in, and before long, I was at the center of the pack and was enjoying myself.

Rhuldan's called out from behind me. "I hate to break up the fun, but our friends are arriving. We should go meet them."

"Hear that pups? I'll have to play some other time." I had to shake my legs to make room to walk. Several of the young grinkuns tried to follow me, but I told them to stay. And to my surprise, they obeyed.

Rhuldan wore a long orange cape, keeping his face and hands covered. He handed me a similar one, but mine was white. "Here, put this on."

"Why are we wearing these?"

"We need to move through the public sectors to get to the docking bay. Some of the more private races wear these in public. Stay close to me, and everyone should think we're a couple."

I rubbed my brow. "Dare I ask which part of the couple I'm supposed to be?"

"Does it matter?"

"I guess not."

"Then follow your husband, one step behind and on the left. Keep your head down and let me do the talking."

"Why can't I be the guy? I'm a migrun pounder, remember?"

"If we get stopped, they won't ask you any questions if they think you are my property."

"Yes dear." I donned the cape and followed him through a passage that opened up into a public hallway. I couldn't see much more than the ground, but I noticed all kinds of alien feet, hooves, wheels, and slimy slug bellies passing by. None seemed to notice me. We arrived at a door just like the one Slowhand had shown me with the warning "Red means dead."

"Here we are." Rhuldan opened the hatch and stepped inside. I followed, closing it behind me.

"Hey look, it's the new guys," Gorthul said. In person, he was slightly shorter than me, but his head was twice the size of mine. I bet he could bite my arm off with a single snap.

Rhuldan removed his hood. "I am Rhuldan, and this is Idiom." He nudged me with his elbow.

I pulled my hood back and nodded. "Good to meet you."

"Jekto! Come here. Look, it's the Migrun Pounder."

The floor vibrated as Jekto approached. Walking on just his back legs, he towered above me by at least a foot. His body was covered with heavy, bony-looking plates, and his horn shined gold. His four upper limbs ended with hands large enough to crush my skull, and by the look of the muscles in his chest and arms, he could do just that without trouble. I'd say he weighed over a thousand pounds. No wonder this guy carried the loot and bashed heads.

"Migrun Pounder! Ha, you look as tiny as one of them," Jekto said.

I'd better play it tough. "Don't let my size fool you. Have you heard what I've done?"

"Beaten up a formation of migrun bare handed."

"I've never seen anyone get up after one of his punches," Rhuldan said.

"Then it's true?" Jekto asked. His breath reeked as he stuck his golden horn close to my face. At this distance, I noticed where it had been broken off at some point and replaced with the yellow metal, like a gold tooth.

"I've got time if you want to find out."

Jekto laughed. The motion made the floor vibrate. "I like this guy, Gorthul. He's got knots." He turned toward Rhuldan. "I'm not touching you."

"You made a wise decision."

Jekto called out, "Hey, robot, meet the new guys."

Dreydus Seven Oh Six disconnected a cable tethering his chest to their ship. His steps were perfectly timed and balanced to be silent on the hard floor. "Acquaintance recorded in registry."

"A pleasure," I said. Their ship was a thing of beauty, black and streamlined like a fish, with what looked like massive cannons mounted on its wingtips, top, front and rear. Compared to Sarge, the only other ship I'd seen, this thing was a work of art.

"That's the *Onyx Infiltrator*," Gorthul said. "You're lucky. Not many have seen her and survived to tell the tale."

"She's quite a beauty."

"That she is. But we're not here to admire my ship. Let's discuss the mission." Gorthul walked toward one wall. The robot projected an image of a planet on it from one of the circles on its "face." "We are heading to Khutanga. The planet has twelve military satellites in orbit. These satellites are equipped with long range scanners to detect any incoming ships, as well as countermeasures to defend against attack." Several red dots appeared above the world, moving in various orbits.

"When you say countermeasures, what does that mean?"

"Missiles with warheads capable of blasting us into atoms."

I nodded. Most of what he said meant nothing to me, but I recognized that he saw it as dangerous. "Ah, countermeasures."

Gorthul said, "Don't fear, they won't detect us before being deactivated. We'll emerge in the system near its sun. They can't monitor vectors directly toward a star as the radiation overwhelms their sensors. We approach the planet on a direct path, and I'll activate stealth systems. We'll use their natural moon…" The image changed to show the planet shrinking, and a moon appeared. "…to further hide from their scans. Once we are on the far side of that moon, we'll deploy a probe. That probe will emit an EMP burst, temporarily blinding the nearest satellite. During that time, we will approach and dock with that satellite, and Dreydus will hack into their system."

"Correct," Dreydus said. "A loss of connection with a single satellite is uncommon but not unheard of. They'll initiate a communication reset, and by the time they're done, the system will be transmitting a replay loop of clear space to all the others. They'll have no idea anything is wrong."

Gorthul smiled an evil grin. "Then we land here, undetected at a natural crater a few miles from the site. We'll be equipped with full breathing apparatus, so we can use gas canisters to dispatch our opposition. Dreydus will open the doors. We'll march through and take out any stragglers or soldiers in gas masks, retrieve our package, and return to Panadara. Dreydus, what are our odds of success?"

"Overall mission success, ninety-two point seven six percent."

"I'll take those odds," I said.

"Great. Now we need to refuel and restock our ship. If you don't have breathing gear, you better get some. Meet back here in six hours."

"Got it." I turned to Rhuldan. "Any clue where we can get breathing gear?"

"There's likely to be a vendor selling salvaged gear somewhere on this rock."

I shrugged. "You do know I have zero credits, right?"

Rhuldan's face faded. "I doubt a merchant would be willing to donate it to the cause."

I sighed. "What are our options?"

"We can see if the grinkun might have something we can use. Since Fayye is funding this operation, she's the most likely to help."

"That will work. Fayye likes me."

"You sure you don't have a thing for her?"

I made a disgusted face. "Seriously? She's not even human! She reminds me of a dog I used to have."

"Interesting."

"What's interesting?"

"Nothing. Let's see if your dog can set us up."

Used grinkun breathing gear smelled of wet dog and bad breath, but, as I was told, it would be better than being knocked unconscious. We tested the equipment several times and, as I was getting hungry again, I packed a bag with several loaves of grinkun bread to take with me.

Rhuldan stuffed his gear into a cloth pack and pulled his cape and hat on. "Nearly six hours have passed. We need to head to the docking bay."

"I'm ready," I said and put my cape on as well. I took a few steps and my stomach roiled painfully. "Oh boy. I need to make a stop along the way."

"What's wrong?"

"I've got a gut full of angry pythons wanting out, pronto."

"I'm just going to have to guess what that means. I'll wait outside the sanitary station. Upwind. I may put on my breathing gear as well."

"Funny. Just help me get there, and I'll be fine in a few minutes." I followed him as my cramps grew more painful, one step behind and just to his left. Finally, I saw the signs

I was beginning to recognize. I found a proper facility, took a seat, and got to work.

I thought I was done several times before another rumble roiled through my stomach and started the process all over again. Rhuldan called out more than once, asking me if I was all right. Finally, I cleaned up, and the entire asteroid jerked to the side as if something serious had just happened. Alarms blared, creatures ran and yelled, too fast to understand. I rushed. "What happened?"

Rhuldan was much too calm for the situation. "Explosion."

"What blew up?"

"I have no idea. Let's get to the docking bay. We need to get out of here, now." He trotted at a pace I could barely keep up with, and on several occasions, I bumped into unnamed critter scurrying to find safety. When we arrived at the bay door, Rhuldan stopped and cursed.

"What is it?"

"Look for yourself."

I pulled my hood back enough to see the red light glowing at the top of door D496. "Red means dead, right?"

"It means the bay is open to space. There's vacuum on the other side of that door. If we're lucky, our new friends bugged out after the explosion."

The floor vibrated as something heavy approached. Jekto bolted toward us like a horse running from lightning. "That was an explosion! Felt like a lektion fusion warhead."

Rhuldan pointed toward the light. "This bay is open to vacuum."

Jekto slammed a foot into the floor. "Then they're dead."

I saw movement in my periphery. "Guys, I hate to break this rendezvous up, but there are guards coming this way."

"We should split up," Rhuldan said. "Meet up together in a safe place."

"Great, any ideas where?" I asked.

"I don't think it's safe to return to Fayye. Odds are, the guards are looking for her."

"Let's all meet up at bay B163," I said.

"What's there?" Rhuldan asked.

"The closest thing I have to friends."

CHAPTER EIGHT
THE RESERVES

I stared at the door, reaching for the handle several times before resting my hand on it. *This is it. Bay B163. What's the worst I can expect? Ginn may be angry, and sure, things went a little sideways, but she'll be understanding. I mean, it's me, and she saved me once, so she must have some reason for it. Just remember to smile a lot, and it will be fine. Better just get it over with.* I opened the door and eased my way inside when something grabbed my arm, pulling me in and throwing me backward. My head smacked against the wall. I saw stars in my blurred vision. Then I noticed the business end of what I assumed was a serious weapon in my face.

"Hands up high. Give me an excuse to wipe that stupid grin off your face with a blast of plasma," Ginn said.

I threw up my hands. "Woah, Ginn, it's me!"

"I know who you are."

That thing looked deadly just by how she was holding it. "Then what's with the gun in my face?"

Ginn raised one eyebrow just a touch. "Did you have anything to do with that explosion?"

"You know I wouldn't have a clue how to do something like that, nor any reason."

"That's true, but you've just made things worse. The migrun are after you, and if they find you here, they'll arrest me as well. So why should I let you live?"

"Now wait a second. Let's just talk about this. Why would you want to kill *me*?"

Ginn's face reddened. "You had one job! Hand over the shade to the migrun, and we'd get paid. What part of that didn't you understand?"

I lowered my hands a little. "Do you remember the part where you said I'd get an image of doom when I approached him. Actually, I had just the opposite sensation. Like I could trust him."

"So you ignored the plan because of a sensation? What if I have a feeling I should blast you?"

I looked her square in the eyes. "Let me ask you. Why did you save me, back on Earth?"

Ginn looked away from me. "A moment of weakness, or perhaps stupidity. Trust it won't happen again."

"I think there's more to it. I think you saved me because I stayed and fought by your side when those men accused you of being a Skinwalker."

Ginn lowered her weapon. Now it pointed at my knees. "Those men were telling their version of the truth."

"That didn't give them a right to murder you in cold blood, without a trial. You knew where I stood on that hill, and you should have known I wouldn't hand over Rhuldan unless I thought he was a threat."

"That is your weakness, not mine," Ginn said.

"I consider it a strength. Besides, they forced my hand by charging in too early. I wanted to talk to him and get his side of things first."

"The migrun aren't known for patience. Apparently, they were able to track the temporal diode and thought you were taking too long. In any case, we broke our deal with them which means they are going to want repayment."

"Repayment? Don't tell me they paid upfront."

"I don't take on jobs like that without collecting half upfront. I used that money to pay off the arenea."

I shrugged. "Well, at least we don't have to worry about the spiders coming after us."

Ginn raised her weapon again, pointing it at my chest. "You don't understand. The arenea are dangerous, but they respect trilatinum. They're likely to give us an opportunity to make financial amends before feeding you to the Mother Spider. But the migrun are brutal, and they call the shots around here. Once they decide we're a liability, we will be dead before we can react."

"I'm not turning Rhuldan over to them. He's only acted to protect himself when attacked. Why do they want him, anyway?"

Ginn turned her head toward the floor. "That's not the type of question you ask the migrun."

"I see. Could we refund their money, with a little bonus to say we're sorry?"

"If we had the credits."

"What if I had a job for us? One that would pay well enough to fix this problem?"

"That would have to be quite a job," Ginn said. She turned her weapon toward the door as it opened.

Jekto stepped in, saw the weapon and raised four limbs into the air. "No need for that," he said.

"And who are you?" Ginn asked.

"I'm Jekto. I'm with him." He pointed toward me.

Ginn stared at me with a look indicating both anger and wonder. "Where did you get a dichelon?"

"It's a long story. Maybe we should wait until Rhuldan gets here."

"The shade is coming here!?"

"Yes."

"This just keeps getting worse." Ginn tapped her wrist twice. "Solondrex, grab a plasma rifle and get out here."

I tried to diffuse the tension. "Let's all relax. There's no reason for weapons."

Jekto looked at me and snorted. "You want me to bash her head good?"

"No. We're all going to talk through this, peacefully."

His hot breath caused the hairs on the back of my neck to stand erect. "I don't like talking."

"Let me handle this. No head bashing." The sound of the door handle turning drew my attention toward it. Fayye entered.

Ginn pointed the weapon toward Fayye. "Who are you and why are you here?"

"He sent for me." She pointed to me.

"What? I didn't send for you," I said.

Fayye stepped toward me. "I received a note from one of our miners. It had this bay number on it and said to meet you here."

"Actually, I sent that note," Rhuldan said as he stepped in behind her. "I thought you might be a target for whoever blew up the docking bay."

Ginn snapped her head toward Rhuldan. "What do you know about the explosion?"

"Nothing, other than it apparently killed our team, with the exception of Jekto here."

Slowhand appeared from inside Sarge. He was carrying a rifle as well. "Who are all you people?"

"This is going to take some explaining. Can we sit and talk?" I said.

Ginn glared at Fayye. "I'll talk, but she needs to turn off the pheromones."

"Feral moans?" I asked.

"She's dripping with them. She's probably using them to control the minds of weaker species. Do they effect you, Idiom? Do you have an urge to please her?"

"No. I mean, I don't know."

Fayye smiled slightly. "I do not have complete control over my pheromones. At least not during this cycle. But I will attempt to tone them down."

"Fine," Ginn said. "Is this everyone, or should I be expecting a crystalline jaguar at the door?"

"This is everyone I know," I said.

After Sarge tried to summon a non-existent security force to lock us all up, I told Ginn, Slowhand, and Sarge everything that had happened to me since I left them. They snickered, laughed, and acted like I was a complete idiot. Fayye explained the details of the job and assured them, if successful, we'd all be reimbursed enough to make our migrun troubles disappear. That is if we were able to complete the job, retrieve the element zero, deliver it to a safe location, and make it back here.

Ginn remained silent, contemplating everything we'd said. She rested an elbow on the table and leaned forward, placing her head against her hand as if in deep thought. She finally raised up and said, "I think the arenea hatching damaged your brain. Have you gone insane?"

Before I could reply, Slowhand said, "That would be a very short trip."

I gave the sloth-cat a nasty look. "I've seen some crazy stuff lately, but as far as I can tell, I'm still in my right mind."

Ginn stood, leaning with her hands on the table. "You want us, without the stealthy ship, and hacking robot, to infiltrate an armed migrun base, to steal back the element zero? That same ore they sent an advanced commando team to retrieve, with orders to kill anybody who got in their way? Then they took it to a facility equipped with automated defenses. You know we're not a militia force, don't you? We run supplies and take on the occasional odd job. Sure, sometimes the things we do might be on the migrun naughty list, but we're not the crew you're looking for. Sorry about your luck, Idiom. Considering how you and your shade friend here are wanted for an assault by the migrun, we just might be able to clear ourselves by turning you two over to them."

"What?!" I shouted. "I fought at your side when those men tried to kill you!"

"And I repaid you by bringing you here and saving your life. That debt has been repaid in full," Ginn said.

"And you don't care that the migrun have the materials to build a weapon able to wipe out an entire world?"

"That's not our concern."

Fayye coughed slightly. "It actually *is* your concern. People ignore the grinkun, leaving us to our mining operations and assuming we're too stupid to get involved with the political posturing aboard this asteroid. But we have connections, as well as an elite force of guards who are capable of swarming this docking bay and eliminating anyone who stands against me."

Ginn slammed a fist on the table. I thought she was ready to attack. "I locked the bay door before we began this discussion! How do you expect your guards to get in here?"

"They had no trouble capturing a shade without incident. We have our ways of getting in and out of areas without detection," Fayye said.

Rhuldan's eyes glowed brightly. "She isn't lying about the fact the grinkun overwhelmed us in an instant. They came from above, below, and behind us, all at once. However, I should add that I was following Idiom's instructions not to kill them. If anyone here tries to turn me over to the migrun, I have no intention to be so compliant."

A chill ran down my spine as the room fell silent. I wanted to say something to diffuse the tension, but nothing came to mind, so I held my hands out in front of me, palms down, and lowered them twice, hoping the action would universally mean "calm down."

Ginn stood from the table, grabbed a glass of something, and sipped the liquid while facing away from us. She returned the drink to the countertop and turned back. "So, it comes down to we die trying to do this stupid mission, or you have your guards kill us right here and now?"

Fayye said, "You assume this is a suicide mission, but I believe it has a reasonable chance of success, considering the intel I've collected. Besides, do you think I'd be joining you if I thought we'd all be killed?"

"What? Do you think you're joining us? I don't think so, sister! Your pheromones have already overtaxed the air scrubbers. I am *not* traveling with a walking hormone emitter!"

Fayye lifted her nose. "What other choices do you have?"

Ginn looked as if she were biting her lip and then turned away.

"Let's say we're successful. What are you offering us?" I asked.

Fayye stretched her back like a cat preening. "I have no interest in ruining my reputation with the migrun. We'll make this look like a pirate operation, and once we've retrieved and returned the ore to a safe location, we'll sell off enough to cover all your expenses and your debt to the migrun, plus a bonus. Say five thousand credits for each of you?"

Slowhand perked his ears up. This was the first time he seemed interested in the conversation. "Five thousand credits? Make it ten thousand, and I'm in."

"If he's getting ten, then I'm getting ten," Ginn replied.

Fayye glanced in my direction. "Equal shares for equal risk," I said.

"Same here," Rhuldan said.

"See? I knew we'd be able to come to an agreement like professionals. It would be wise for us to launch soon."

"Wait," Ginn said, staring down Fayye. "That explosion. What do you know about it?"

Fayye talked through gritted teeth. "I certainly had no involvement, if that's your question. I spent a lot of credits just to get them here. Those mercenaries had made a lot of enemies over the cycles. My best guess is someone recognized them or their ship and decided to take them out. I imagine the authorities were willing to pay well for that."

"You swear you had nothing to do with it?" I asked.

"That explosion put this entire mission in jeopardy. Trust me, when I find out who was responsible, I will make them pay." Fayye tightened a paw into a fist.

I stood and leaned against the table. "Whoever did it is still out there, and if they connect us to that team, we could be next. Keep in mind, Jekto is with us, and, no offense, but he arrived with them, so if he's a target, we are too."

Jekto puffed out his chest, growling like an angry badger. "If anyone is brave enough to come after me, I pity their next of kin who tries to identify their remains! That goes for any of you if you think I was involved. Those people were my friends."

"Easy, big fellow. Nobody is accusing you of anything," I said. "I'm just saying we may be safer for the time being, away from here."

Jekto crossed his four arms. "Then we launch."

"You heard the man," I said, immediately regretting it.

Ginn wagged a finger in my face. "You don't make that call. I do."

I nodded in agreement. "My apologies. I just think we all agree waiting around to see if the migrun try to pin this on us is a bad idea."

Ginn paced around the room several times. She stopped and said, "I've made my decision."

"What's your call?" I asked.

"I expect we're going to regret this, but we launch," Ginn said. "We'll work on a plan while we travel. If any of you cause trouble, I'm not above spacing you."

Everyone but Jekto and I left the room. "Is that bad?"

"Spacing? Yes, that's bad. How long can you live without an atmosphere?"

"I have no idea. Maybe a minute."

"That's because your skin is like paper. Dichelon skin is tough. My people have stories of our warriors floating for days in space before being found. No long-term effects, other than their nails turned purple."

"Don't you need to breathe?"

"My ancestors had to survive on a world with a thin atmosphere and strong storms. We auto-hibernate when air pressure drops to dangerous levels."

That could certainly come in handy. The rest of the crew had wandered off to find bunks or areas to claim as their own. My thoughts went back to Ginn and Jekto meeting. "Let me ask you. Would Ginn's gun kill you?"

"Not likely. It'd take several shots to penetrate my hide. If I were dumb enough to show her the same side as she was firing, I'd deserve death."

"Lucky you. What do you think it would do to me?"

"Hard to say. You probably have a similar build to a holtian. I've seen a plasma gun remove a Holtian's head once. I never laughed so hard in my life. It stood there convulsing for a solid ten seconds before falling over!" Jekto laughed and acted like his hands were searching for a missing head.

"That's comforting," I said.

"There are worse ways to die. Get me drunk some time, and I'll tell you about them." He walked away from me, turning back as he reached the doorway. "I hope they have something to eat on this barge. That and a bathroom properly equipped for me. Otherwise, things could get ugly."

"Do I want to know?"

Jekto raised his head up proud and high. "Round pellets. Thirty pounds or more apiece, dense as a stone."

"You could hurt somebody with one of those. That or yourself." Jekto walked off without a response. I tried in vain to get the image of him crapping a cannonball out of my mind, wondering if he was serious or not. I did some quick estimates of his size compared to my own and what I've seen a buffalo leave behind and concluded he wasn't joking. Thankfully, Rhuldan appeared at the doorway.

"Are you all right? You have a pained look on your face," he asked.

"Nothing like I imagine Jekto gets."

"What?"

"He told me he makes thirty-pound pellets."

"Yes. Dichelon's are legendary for that. The bigger the droppings, the higher the pecking order in their society. That size would put him high in the hierarchy."

I rubbed my head. "Do they have some official measuring system?"

"It goes by weight, or so I hear," Rhuldan said. "This is grade-school stuff. Didn't they teach you the basics?"

"Apparently not."

"Have you found your bunk?"

"Haven't left this room."

"Follow me. There's a free room next to mine. It's not first class, but it beats the grinkun dungeon." He showed me to a doorway with rounded edges and a heavy latch.

As he opened the entrance, sealed released and air hissed. I was surprised to see how thick the door was. *Are all the doors here airtight?* I walked inside to find a flat bed with a padded cushion, a bench I couldn't move sitting before a table that folded out from one wall, another wall was completely reflective like the finest mirror.

Rhuldan pressed a button on the side of the bed, and the top lifted, providing access to a storage area underneath. He then turned to the mirrored wall and said, "Current events." The mirror changed into a screen displaying dozens of moving images, each accompanied by someone speaking about what was happening. I saw ships launching and aliens talking about them and how the war was affecting supplies in various sectors. I couldn't comprehend all the information I was seeing, and I was overwhelmed, like a hundred people were talking to me at once.

He pointed to one of the pictures and then moved his hands apart. That section expanded in size and filled the entire wall. A gray scaled turtle talked about a battle somewhere and how the migrun were making headway every day to eliminate the crystalline threat. Rhuldan watched for a moment and shook his head without making a sound. I saw concern in his eyes for an instant. He made a hand motion at the screen, and a new image replaced the news report. Two aliens who looked like furry puppets with eyes glued to the top of their heads started talking about getting along with your neighbors.

"What is this?" I asked.

"It's a program for the kids. You should watch it. It will teach you a lot about our society, and the songs are catchy. You can pause the program by holding your palm up toward the screen. To start it, move your finger quickly from left to right. I'm going to work on some ideas to keep us from getting killed during this job."

"Thanks," I said. I sat down to watch a green, four-eyed puppet try to steal a red furry slug's food before getting blasted into a pile of smoking rubble, then he rematerialized, and they sang happily together:

Never walk behind a flatulon if you have a sense of smell,
Never deal with a dracnarian — you'll know not what you sell.
When you eat or drink or defecate, remember: wash your hands,
Always bring your space suit, when you visit foreign lands.

Most people don't like snitches, parasites or lice,
When you speak with your elders, remember to be nice.
The migrun are our protectors against the crystal blight,
If you steal somebody's cookies, be ready for a fight.

For the next several days, we traveled inside this ship called Sarge. I explored every area I was allowed inside, but I found a few doors I couldn't open. I assumed there was a reason they didn't want me in the "fusion reactor," so I didn't push my luck.

Fayye, Rhuldan, and Ginn met for several hours a day discussing tactics. Slowhand mostly slept, hanging upside down from a horizontal bar near the cockpit, and Jekto kept to himself, eating like a platoon of soldiers who'd just marched double-time for a month. That boy could eat.

I tried to follow the conversations and the ways they thought they could infiltrate the migrun base. Every plan seemed to end up in at least one of the three of them saying, "This is a suicide mission."

I sensed Ginn was avoiding me, for whatever reason, but I wasn't exactly going out of my way to be around her, either. I went to my bunk and watched several hours of puppets telling me not to lick a slime trail, what constituted a "bad touch," and why I should always look both right and left before crossing a transit track. I was bored out of my gourd, so I paused the program and tried something. "Hey, Sarge, can you hear me?"

"Five by five, soldier. What is your need?"

I had trouble knowing where to look while talking to Sarge, so I just spoke up like I was talking to God. "Just needed someone to talk to. Do you have a minute?"

"I have lots of minutes. I'm capable of concurrently carrying dozens of conversations without diminishing my ability to run the ship. What do you want to talk about, Private Lee?"

"Have you been listening in on the team working on tactics?"

"They have the Situation Room set to cloistered mode. I cannot listen in there."

I noticed his voice sounded like it was coming from a panel with dozens of holes in it, so I spoke to that. "But surely the conversation has carried on outside of that room."

"Aye, it has, Private. I've picked up a few bits and pieces."

"Are you familiar with the target location?"

"Refinery base Khutanga."

"Yes. Do you know anything about it?"

"Just the normal statistics. I haven't intercepted any unusual communications from them."

"Wait, you can listen to them too?"

"Of course. I have the highest level of migrun clearance. Just this morning, I picked up a message they were having difficulty with their waste treatment facility. A team of two nebatian repair engineers were requested. Their ship is several days out."

I pressed two fingers on the panel he spoke from. "Sarge, you are like finding a vein of gold in a silver mine. If you had a face, I'd kiss you!"

"Hey, now, none of that talk is allowed in this man's army. But I'm glad I could be of assistance. I hope this mission aids in our efforts to kick some crystal skulls!"

"Me too," I said before running to find the crew. I found Jekto in the mess with a pile of something orange and chunky sitting on a platter before him. "Come to the Situation Room. I have our answer."

Jekto raised one eyebrow toward me, shrugged, and shoveled food into his mouth. Orange gobs dribbled down his chin as a huge tongue circled his lips to snatch any remaining morsels. Some of the goo dripped from his golden horn, and he didn't seem to notice or care.

I found Slowhand hanging from his perch in the cockpit. "Hey, Slowhand, come with me. I have our answer."

Slowhand opened one eye just a sliver. With the speed of a dying turtle, he raised a middle finger in the air. The message was clear.

"Fine. You'll find out later, you lazy sloth." I left him there. Everyone else argued around the table. Plans had been written on glass-like boards and crossed out multiple times, and someone had drawn dead bodies in fine detail next to several options. Fayye stood toe to toe with Ginn, both of them speaking faster than I could follow and in tones to send a chill down my spine. Rhuldan had a look of disgust on his face that made me wonder if he might kill both of them, just for some peace and quiet.

"Excuse me," I said. Nobody responded. I doubt they could even hear me. I glanced over to see Jekto watching me. He had a dopey-looking grin on his face, the orange goo still on the side of his golden horn. I pointed toward it and made a motion of wiping the side of my own nose. He didn't understand my pantomime, so I shrugged and walked toward Ginn and Fayye, placing a hand on each one's shoulders, pushing them apart. "Ladies, I said excuse me." A silence fell upon the room. It was the quiet you hear just before a gunfight begins. I knew I had to talk fast. "I have our solution."

"You have our solution?" Ginn asked. "Unless it involves you and all your friends volunteering to space yourselves, I sincerely doubt it's worth listening to."

"Give him a chance," Fayye said.

"Thank you. Now I don't pretend to understand what Sarge is, but somehow, he's able to listen in on the base we're trying to infiltrate."

Ginn crossed her arms. "That's impossible."

"Then explain how he knew they had just requested an engineering team to repair their waste systems. He said something about having the highest level migrun clearance, and two nednations are on their way to fix it. Something like that."

Rhuldan shook a bony finger in the air. "Ginn, it's time to come clean about Sarge. Where did he come from?"

Ginn's face paled, and she sighed. "Fine. We're already in over our heads. When Solondrex and I were putting together this ship, we needed an A.I. to run it. We couldn't find one capable for what we needed on the open markets..."

Rhuldan said, interrupting, "I'm assuming you mean the black markets?"

"Yes. Everyone knows trading in A.I.s is prohibited. We had the ship pieced together, but it wasn't space worthy without an advanced controller. We ran multiple simulations trying to control the ship manually. We could fly it for a while and even land it. But we needed a ship to make Null Space jumps. Without an A.I. to make those calculations, we were more likely than not to die on our first jump. Then we got word of a destroyed migrun dreadnought, the *Zammarius*. It had been damaged beyond repair in a border skirmish, and the migrun towed it to one of their junkyard asteroids. We hired on as temporary scrappers until one day, Solondrex was able to phase shift himself aboard the ship when no one was looking. We stole the A.I. canister, snuck it into our personal cases, got ourselves fired for insubordination and sent back to Panadaras."

"And you installed this illegally obtained A.I. into this ship," Rhuldan said. "Which would incur a penalty of no less than death, if caught."

"No less than death?" I replied. "What's worse than death?"

Rhuldan's eyes squinted a dire warning. "The migrun can be quite creative when it comes to punishment. Trust me, they have penalties worse than death."

"Their penalties are only a concern if we get caught, and I don't intend for that to happen," Ginn said.

"You realize that each of us, just by being aboard this vessel, would be considered guilty of high crimes against the migrun, don't you?" Rhuldan asked.

Ginn's voice softened. "Solondrex and I did what we had to do. Besides, we didn't invite any of you aboard, remember?"

"Understood. In any case, there's nothing we can do about it at the moment. Meantime, can someone explain to me Sarge's memory problems?" I asked.

"A dreadnought class destroyer has memory banks as large as this entire ship. Sarge's system controls and personality are hardcoded. Depending upon how much data he's processing, his short-term memory can last for a dozen or so minutes, to a little over an hour. Solondrex has grafted into his system an identity file for each of us, so he doesn't try to attack us every time we board. Other than that, he can't remember much of anything."

Jekto grunted. "This is getting boring. The solution is simple. We intercept the engineer's ship coming to fix their waste system, and we take their ship and their places. That gets us on the base without being shot down. Once inside, we bash skulls together, take the prize, and leave the system. It'll be fun."

"Let's try it with a little more finesse, but the general plan is solid," Fayye said.

"How do we intercept the other ship?" I asked.

Ginn spoke like she was trying to convince herself. "If Sarge still has the clearance you said he does, we can have him summon them to us with military override authority. We'll work through the details, but this is the best plan we've got. There's a good chance some of us might survive it."

Something moved behind me. Slowhand peeked into the room, his fur flattened on one side like he had bed-head all across his body. "What did I miss?"

"Just this." I raised a single finger in his direction.

CHAPTER NINE
ENGINEERING DUTY

Finn grabbed my arm, holding it under some cylindrical device that looked torturous as if it might crush the bone if tightened too much. "Hold still. This will sting just a little."

"What is it going to do?"

"It's a smart ink printer. You haven't been imprinted before, so if you're going to be part of the team, you need this and a few other additions."

"Additions?"

"Relax. Now turn your wrist up."

The device clamped down on my arm so hard, I couldn't have moved it if I'd wanted to. I felt a strange burning sensation as if thousands of tiny needles were puncturing my skin. I gritted my teeth, trying to hold back any sign of pain or fear. The pain finally stopped, the clamps released, and my arm had a small black band tattooed on it. "What the hell? Why did you have to brand me?"

"You aren't branded. Just watch." The black disappeared from my sight.

"Neat trick. Is there a reason for it?"

"Just wait. Now hold still while I inject you a couple of times. First, let me see your ear." She pulled a tubular device from a toolkit and touched a few buttons on it. A light came on the device. She inserted it into my ear, and I felt a sharp pinch. She replaced the tip, and repeated the procedure, but this time in my cheek.

"What's with the doctor's exam?"

"I've implanted two transceivers in you. Let's test them." She touched my arm where the black band had been, and words appeared in multiple colors on my arm. Ginn touched the word "Comms," and a list of names appeared. When she saw her own, she pressed it and the words turned a bright green color. "Wait until I leave, then talk." She walked out of the room.

"What should I talk about? How I don't enjoy being poked and prodded?"

"You're coming in clear," Ginn's voice sounded as if she were right beside me. I turned to see if she'd snuck up on me, but she was nowhere to be found. "Where are you?"

"I'm in the cockpit. Solondrex has a message for you. Oh, I can't translate that into words."

"Yeah, tell him he can do the same to himself."

"You can tell him that. Press your arm as I did and select his name. If both names are highlighted, you're talking to both of us. If only one is outlined, you're only talking to that individual."

"Ahoy, Slowhand. Are you there?"

He sighed loudly. "Unfortunately, yes."

"One of these days I'm going to teach you a lesson about rude gestures."

"Try it, and I'll phase you into the wall."

"Can you phase a forty-five caliber slug of lead out of the air?"

"Point taken. Now leave me alone unless you have something important to discuss."

"Bye," I said, pressing his name on my arm, the color changed from green to gray. "Just testing," she said.

"I can hear you fine."

"Good. This tech is uncommon out here."

"By uncommon, can I assume it's stolen?" I asked.

Ginn didn't answer my question, so I assumed the worst. "Just don't show it off and you'll be fine. Wait where you are. I'll come back. to you."

I touched my arm where I'd been tattooed to see different words and pictures appear. *This is some kind of magic!*

Ginn returned. She seemed to smile as she watched me messing with my arm. "Sarge has some new information on the engineering team. We've confirmed they are expecting two nebatians. That is both good and bad news for us. The bad news is only two of us can get inside. Good news is, nebatians are bipedal chlorine breathers, so they have to wear full EVA suits any time they are working in a migrun environment."

"And that means to me?"

"Once you're inside one of their suits, nobody will recognize you."

I cleared my throat. "I see. So, I'm on this engineering team. Who else?"

"Rhuldan. We send you both in because you are the most qualified for the job."

I raised an eyebrow. "How could that be possible? Me being most qualified for any job out here?"

Ginn gave me a dismissive wave of her hand. "You can shovel waste, can't you? Nine times out of ten, someone has flushed something they shouldn't have into the waste collectors, and it's jammed the filters. Your job is to drain the tank, shovel away whatever you find stuck in the grate, and pack it into a containment cell. While you're doing that, Rhuldan will search the station to determine where they are keeping the ore."

"This sounds like a terrible job."

"That's why we picked you. The vote was unanimous."

"I don't recall voting."

"Only you, me, and Rhuldan can fit in a nebatian's suit. I'm needed here in case something goes wrong, so the choice was clear."

I laughed. "Can I guess that something is to run away if we get caught?"

"I'd call it a strategic retreat, but maybe you are smarter than you look, Idiom." Ginn's lip curled into a smile that bordered on sardonic and stopped at mocking. "When Rhuldan locates the element zero, he'll let us all know where it is. Then you'll need to create a distraction. We slip in, Jekto grabs our prize, and we sneak away."

I raised one palm into the air in a questioning fashion. "How am I supposed to create this distraction?"

"That will be up to you. We don't know where the ore will be stored, so I can't tell you the best way to handle it. You'll have to think on your feet."

"Fine. I'll figure out something. Can I ask you something in the meantime?"

"What is it?"

I steeled my nerves, but my voice still squeaked a little when I asked, "I hope this isn't too personal, but I have to know. How do you turn into that beast?"

Ginn placed both hands on her hips. "You're not going to let this go, are you?"

"Indulge my curiosity. Besides, I'll likely get killed down there, so what does it hurt?"

Ginn's face turned dour. "You could not pronounce my species name. It's forty-seven syllables and required three sets of vocal cords to say it properly. In any case, we have two forms — our relaxed state, as you see me now, and our predator form. About once every four of your Earth weeks, a hunger grows within my stomach and my psyche. When this happens, I must hunt. I can fight the urge for a few days, but if I attempt to delay the transformation for too long, it can cause... issues."

I took a step back. "By issues do you mean you might attack your crewmates?"

"That is a possible side effect."

I coughed quietly. "I'll keep that in mind."

"You're safe for the time being. Solondrex helps me find primitive worlds within our range for me to hunt on."

"Like Earth? We're not that primitive."

Ginn laughed, shook her head, and made a tssk sound. "Earth is about a week past living in caves and fighting with sticks. In fact, some of your people still do those things."

"Believe what you want. One thing doesn't add up though. When we met the first time, you attacked my horse, and you must have eaten him. I liked that horse, by the way."

"Sorry. If it helps, he gave me indigestion."

I frowned. "No, that doesn't help at all. His name was Leroy, and I'd had him for three years."

"I didn't know he was your pet. I thought he was wild, like a deer."

"He had a saddle on him and I was riding him! How could you think he was wild?"

Ginn glanced toward her feet. "I got caught up in the moment."

"It's over now. But how could you have still been hungry after eating a horse when those men were attacking us?"

Ginn looked back at me. "I wasn't hungry. I was angry."

"I see. So, you can change when angry as well? How about frustrated or annoyed?"

"If I could change when annoyed, you'd be in real danger, Idiom."

I smiled, hoping she was joking. "I get the sense this isn't common."

"It isn't. My people have legends of our ancestors changing forms to rush into battle, but that ability disappeared centuries ago when we became civilized."

"Yet you were able to do it."

"And that is a secret you must keep. I've been thinking about the migrun and why they wanted Rhuldan."

I raised an eyebrow. "Why do you think they were after him?"

"Probably the same reason they wanted the element zero, to weaponize his abilities. If they knew I had control over my transformation, they'd want me too."

"Your secret is safe with me." My eyes grew heavy, so I made my way back to my bunk.

In the haze of a dream, I recognized the cabin as my home from long ago, my mind content to ignore the inconsistencies and shifting elements as I moved through the place. A man I once looked up to, my father, Brian Dean Lee, sat in a wooden chair, leaning to his right as if he were about to fall to the floor. Now a broken man, thin and weak, content to sit in filthy clothes and stare out a window for hours on end. Dozens of bottles of laudanum littered the room. They had been dropped when emptied and left wherever they landed or rolled.

I gathered up several and set them on the table, making more noise than needed. "Dad, you're killing yourself with this stuff."

His eyes seemed to look through me. "Don't you take my medicine, Idiom Justus Lee."

"I'm not taking your medicine, Dad. This bottle's empty anyway."

"Because you stole it."

"I don't want it. Don't you understand?"

"You're just like your mother." He shook a crooked finger at me. "You and her are working together, aren't you?"

"Dad, Mom's been dead for ten years now. You just can't remember anything 'cause you're in a drug haze all the time. Why do you need this stuff, anyway?"

"You didn't see what I saw. You haven't experience the agony I did." He looked down to where his right foot had once been. Now his pant leg was pinned together a few inches below his knee. "Unless you fought at the Battle of Little Blue River, you have no right to judge me."

"Dad, I was three years old at the time. You'd remember that if you didn't drink this junk all the time."

Dad's eyes cut me down. "What do you want, anyway?"

"What do I want? I've told you several times now that I'm leaving for the Washington University School of Law in Missouri. I was hoping you wouldn't kill yourself before I got there."

"You're leaving me? After the sacrifices I've made for my country? Shows the respect your momma should've taught you while I was away." His face turned into a scowl as evil as Scratch's gaze. It seemed normal to me.

"If I cared what you thought that might bother me. Enjoy your laudanum and staring out your window."

Dad's face turned white as if he'd seen a ghost or was becoming one. "Wait!" He shuffled over to a cabinet, leaning heavily on a pair of wooden crutches. He rummaged through cluttered junk. "Here. Take this with you, Idiom."

"It's a feather, Dad. Why do I need it?"

"It's a golden feather. As long as you have it, it means you'll find your way back home."

"This sound like some of that heathen Indian garbage."

"Just take it."

"Fine. I'll take your feather. Now I'm leaving. I'll ask the Harrisons to check in on you." I glanced over to a table to see my copy of a pocket Bible sitting under a kerosene lantern. I grabbed the book and placed it in my vest pocket. *Someday, I'll read this, I promise.*

"Just leave, Idiom. I'm not worth staying for, anyway."

"Goodbye, Dad." I walked to the door, opening it to a powerful gust of wind. The feather flew from my hand over the cabin. As it fluttered through the air, it screamed a painful wail.

I startled myself awake, took a deep breath and remembered where I was. A sense of isolation overcame me, so I opened the Bible and try to read it a little more. Upon opening it, the Western Union Telegram I'd kept all these years fell to the floor.

I'd read it a hundred times at least, but I couldn't stop myself from reading it once again:

DE DENVER CO   5 32 PM MARCH 15 1892

MR IDIOM LEE

REGRET TO INFORM YOU OF THE PASSING OF BRIAN DEAN LEE

PLEASE VISIT OFFICE AT 113 LARIMER ST TO SETTLE AFFAIRS

REGARDS   PHILIP MORGAN ATTY

I should have gone when I had the chance. Sorry, Dad.

Sarge interrupted my thought. "Private Lee, report to the Situation Room immediately."

"On my way." I blinked a few times, gathered what few wits I had remaining, and followed his instructions, to find our "crew" waiting. Slowhand gave me a sly look as if they had all been there a long time. I shrugged, found a seat, and planted myself in it. "What's the news?"

Ginn made a hand gesture toward the table. An image of a cylinder with multiple tubes, connectors, and strange shapes attached to it. "This is the Gerrund station. Sarge intercepted a docking clearance request from the engineering team. If they follow standard protocols, they'll refuel and resupply there before proceeding to the base. Sarge is calculating the Null Space Conduit to get us there."

"Null Space? You've used those words before. What do they mean?" I asked.

Ginn sighed and rolled her eyes. "It's how we travel great distances."

"You'll always remember your first passage through Null Space," Slowhand said. "The terror often fades after a few years. Of course, some lower species aren't able to survive the trip as it's too much for their primitive brains to process."

"Next you're going to tell me all about the snipe we're hunting," I said. "You're not going to scare me."

"I'll have Sarge record your screams. It will be fun to listen to them while we have snacks." Slowhand's lips curled into an evil smile.

Ginn gave Slowhand a glance that I like to think meant "cut the chatter" but may have been more along the lines of "you're scaring him." "We're ready, Sarge."

"Prepare for Null Space," Sarge said. "In three, two, one…"

If you've never traveled through Null Space, you won't have a true knowledge of how disruptive it is. It started as a tingling sensation at my feet and hands, almost a tickle at first. Then it became painful as if I was being stretched on a medieval rack. The stretching continued until it seemed like my toes were miles away from my head, and everything I'd ever learned raced through my mind. I couldn't see, but images flashed before me, the most memorable being the worst things I had experienced. Leroy being attacked, Ginn as a beast coming toward me, my father slowly killing himself with laudanum, watching my mother die of pneumonia while I held her hand. Fear and sadness. I tried not to scream, but I can't swear I didn't. Then with a sense of ultimate relief, all the pain ended. The absence of agony sent a wave of euphoria through my body as a release beyond words. When my vision returned, Ginn, Fayye, Slowhand, Rhuldan, and Jekto stood before me, and I felt a deep kinship with each of them as if we were now one big, happy family.

"You cried like a little pup," Slowhand said, attempting to spoil the moment.

"I love you guys," I said, sounding like a drunken miner spending his haul on whiskey, women, and song.

"Great, he's one of those," Slowhand replied. "The feeling isn't mutual, I can assure you."

"Don't be a silly kitty. You know you love me." I patted his head like he was a kitten. He bared his teeth, snapping at me.

"Are you done?" Ginn asked.

"Yes," I replied.

"We'll be docking in a few minutes. You and Rhuldan need to get aboard that ship. Your targets are located in bay K-79. We'll be docking in bay W-113. We need to refuel and restock as well, and we have some items in our cargo hold we can sell if the going price is fair. Whoever locates the nebatian engineers needs to let others know their location. Otherwise, let's keep the comms to a minimum. They are supposed to be secure, but lots of things aren't what they should to be."

"Got it," I said. Rhuldan and I returned to our individual quarters, and once again we donned our costumes covering our entire bodies.

"Are you ready?" Rhuldan asked.

"As ready as I can be. What's your plan?"

"I say we make our way toward their ship. We'll scout it out, see what security they have in place, and if we can slip aboard without incident, we do so."

"Do you think we can be so lucky?"

Rhuldan shook his head. "Not a chance. But it's a starting place."

"What do you know about the nebatians?" I asked.

"Not much. You know you can look them up in the galactic encyclopedia, right?"

"What? How?"

"The smart ink on your arm. Go to the search box, type in 'nebatian' and see what it tells you."

I did as he said. A message appeared on my arm saying, "Are you lonely on the Gerrund station? Nebatian females await you!" An image appeared of something green, covered in slime, and moving rhythmically. "What is that?!" I showed my arm to Rhuldan.

"Oh. I'll show you later how to filter your results."

"Please do. That thing looked like a frog had a cold."

"Uh… Never mind, Idiom." The ship shook. "We've docked. Follow me." Rhuldan lead me into a room where hot air blew from the floor, and bright lights burned my eyes. When it stopped, he began walking again.

"What was that?" I asked.

"Decontamination. They don't want you bringing any dangerous germs, parasites or spores on board. It's standard procedure."

"I have a lot to learn about standard procedures."

"Now be quiet. Let's find that ship." He led the way up several ramps and around multiple turns. I wondered how he knew where he was going, but I kept my question to myself. I watched feet of various designs pass by me, as well as a few aliens who didn't bother with touching the floor to move about. At one juncture, what had to be a form of music played from a side room, but to my ears, it sounded as if someone were repeatedly punching a pig in the kidneys. Whatever this music was called, I didn't care for it.

Rhuldan stopped at what I now recognized as an airlock door. He tried the handle twice. "Why couldn't they have left the door open?"

A voice sounded from behind me, sounding strangely mechanical, wet and angry. "What are you doing?"

I held my hands outward to show I wasn't armed as I faced two creatures in fully sealed suits. Their faces were hidden behind reflective glass in their helmets. Nebatians, I was certain. They'd caught us trying to open the door to their docking bay.

Rhuldan whispered, "How do you want to handle this?"

"I have an idea." I was surprised I did.

The pair of engineers approached us, each with a hand over some form of pistol. I raised my hands slowly, glanced down. The slimy frog image still rested on my arm. Without saying a word, I raised my arm up toward the two nebatians, displaying it to them. Then I pointed to the airlock door.

The closest nebatian made a loud, gurgling "Whoa!" sound before stepping past me. He opened the door. We followed them inside and waited for the door to close behind us.

"On three," I whispered to Rhuldan. "One… two… three." We both attacked at the same moment. I grabbed the nearest engineer by the arm, and spun him around, smacking him into the door frame. He fell flat on the floor, unmoving. By the time I turned to see Rhuldan, he had his nebatian by the shoulder, and with a quick spin, the creature's helmet flew off. I smelled a strong odor of chlorine as the alien fell to his knees and gasped for breath, his mouth open wide like a green donut surrounded by quills.

"Let's drag them to their ship. They're bound to have backup suits." Rhuldan pulled his guy by the ankle to a ship smaller than Sarge and sleeker in design, looking more like a flowing piece of polished art than a manufactured vehicle. I followed, dragging my own unconscious fellow. Rhuldan found a breathing mask mounted inside the ship and strapped it to the grotesque face before him.

The nebatian breathed deeply of the chlorine gas. "What do you want with us?" His voice sounded like how I'd imagine a talking cobra might speak — hateful and poisonous.

"We need your ship," Rhuldan said.

"It's nothing personal," I added.

"This is a high crime against the migrun militia. You will suffer slow molecular disruption and reconstruction for years!"

I smiled. "Only if we get caught."

As I studied the alien's space suit, a loud beep sounded in my ear.

I recognized Ginn's voice. "Still no sign of the nebatians. Have you had any luck?"

"We've secured their ship," I said.

"What? How? Why didn't you let us know?"

"Things happened fast. I'll tell you all about it later. We need you to grab a couple of things for us though."

"What do you need?"

"You'll see them when you launch."

"What did you do, Idiom?"

"We released the nebatians."

"Are you an idiot? They'll run straight to the authorities."

"They're not running anywhere, at least not for some time."

Ginn sounded irate, her words over-annunciated. "Where did you release them?"

"To space. Don't worry, they are in their EVA suits, and we smashed their comms. Rhuldan says they're now orbiting the station. Pick them up and leave them in the airlock. Don't let them see you, and take them somewhere safe but unable to contact the migrun."

"When this is over, I want a detailed report of how you did this."

"Aye, Captain. We're heading to Khutanga. We'll contact you when we're ready for a pickup."

"Captain? Hmm, I like the sound of that," Ginn said, before disconnecting.

"What have I started?" I said aloud to myself. Rhuldan was in the cockpit of this ship, working controls I couldn't guess their function.

He glanced over as I entered. "Good news. The engineers already had their destination programmed into the ship, along with their clearance codes. Once we get to the base, the ship should automatically communicate with landing control, and we should go unchallenged."

"I'm not about to say I have a good feeling about this. Let's just knock on wood and hope for the best." I rapped my knuckles on a wall that clearly wasn't made from a tree.

"Knock on wood?"

"It's an old Earth superstition. I don't know where it started, but it is supposed to bring luck."

"I'm not a real believer in luck. Things happen, good or bad, based upon chance and the odds of the occurrence."

"Have you ever seen someone draw to an inside straight? If you can do that, you're lucky in my book," I said.

Rhuldan made a tiny adjustment to a control knob before responding. "Ah, yes, the inside straight in poker. It sounds like it would be nearly impossible to draw, but the real odds are four in forty-seven."

"How do you figure that?"

"There are fifty-two cards in a deck, and you are dealt five. There are forty-seven cards remaining either in the deck or the other players' hands, and four of those cards will complete your straight. About one time in eleven attempts, you'll get the card you need. Try it often enough, and you're bound to get a winner."

I looked at him square in his strangely glowing eyes. "You can do those calculations in your head? Without a pencil and paper?"

"Yes. My species excels in mathematics, algebra, calculus and combinatorics."

"So those last three are like hard math? Harder than fractions?"

"Precisely."

I squinted at Rhuldan, deep in thought. "Can you figure out the odds of our success with this mission, as that mechanical fellow did?"

"He had the advantage of knowing his team's previous success rate. Since this is our first job, I don't have all the data."

I tried to study his face. All I saw was clouds of dark smoke. "What does your gut tell you? What are our odds here?"

"About the same as drawing to an inside straight."

"Sounds about right." I stared out the window, amazed at the display of millions of points of light, each a star, likely surrounded by planets. Bands of colors filled sections of my view creating a beautiful tapestry to study. Considering how many alien species I'd met it just a few days, I had to assume life was rampant out here. What happens when one form of life first meets another? If it's anything like Earth, the stronger people would overtake the weaker ones with little concern.

"Rhuldan, can I ask you something?"

"Sure, if it's not too personal."

"What do you know about the crystal threat?"

"Not a lot. The migrun have been fighting territorial wars with them for years, but little information ever gets released to the public. We get artists renditions of what they believe these creatures look like, but never an actual image. Publicly, the migrun release vague news of regaining territories or minor victories in battle, but I suspect they aren't faring as well as they let on."

I sat in a heavily padded blue seat fitted with multiple straps. It bounced like a spring loaded wagon bench under my weight and then it became hard, not moving at all. "Why do you think that?"

"The migrun are brutal, efficient, and ruthless. They wouldn't allow an attack to occur without immediate retaliation if they had the capability of striking back. When I hear news of them taking back a territory, I expect that region has been stripped of anything of value, and they were allowed to have it."

"Then are we doing the right thing here? If they're trying to protect the galaxy from a bigger threat, perhaps we should allow them to keep this weapon?"

Rhuldan pressed his hands flat together almost as if he were praying. "You've been watching that kid's program, which is teaching you a lot, but you have to understand its bias. The migrun control what is said about them, at least through the official channels. They have no interest in making the galaxy a safe place for everyone. They may be the single most powerful species out here, but there are dozens of other species capable of making things very difficult for them. If two or three of them decided to combine forces, the migrun could be overtaken."

"Would they use the weapon against the other races?"

Rhuldan looked me in the eyes. As his face became clear to see, it appeared more skeletal than I'd remembered. He reminded me of the Grim Reaper when he said, "In my experience, peace is an unnatural state of affairs. There are brief moments in time when everyone tires of war, but those instances are soon replaced by someone's ambitions, fear, or hatred. War is inevitable. If a people don't have an external enemy to fight, they'll find an internal one. It's just the way of the universe."

What a disturbing thought. But is it true? Can any of us find a way to overcome our own instincts?

"You look to be lost in thought," Rhuldan said.

"Just thinking about what you just said. I like to hope there is a chance for lasting peace."

"Hope is a lot like luck. It's an ideology that rarely pans out."

I reached into my vest pocket and felt the Bible I kept there. "I've never been much of a praying man, but it seems to me that a wise man should pray for peace and prepare for war."

Rhuldan gave me a puzzled look followed by complete silence. I turned to look out the window again. If I'd ever learned to paint, I would have painted that view.

There were restrictions related to where we could make a Null Space jump that Rhuldan understood but made little sense to me. The best I could gather is there were too many obstacles between the Gerrund station and Khutanga to allow us a fast passage with a reasonable level of safety and not destroying ourselves and perhaps entire civilizations. That meant we had to travel using what he called Trad-Prop, so we had several days to kill before we'd arrive.

The ship was small by Sarge's standard, but big enough for the two of us to each have a place to eat, sleep, and take care of our private functions. I never expected to say I missed grinkun bread, but the food dispensers here had been calibrated for nebatian needs. Rhuldan worked some chemistry magic to lower the chlorine content to a tolerable level, but everything still tasted awful, and my burps smelled like bleach and made my eyes water. Oddly, Rhuldan didn't seem to be bothered by the food.

Ginn contacted us confirming they'd safely picked up the two nebatians we'd spaced and had delivered them to a distant grinkun settlement lacking in communication tools, but rich in corrosive chemicals. They'd have to work for their food and lodging, but there they could live out their days in peace. From what I'd seen since leaving Earth, that was about as fair a deal they could ask for.

Rhuldan set up what he called a "virtual training system." A projection of a tall, blue, fishlike alien served as my instructor, and it was able to adjust its lessons to me. The classes started with "Waste Treatment Systems for Beginners" and ended with "Advanced Bioaugmentation of Waste Water Systems." Much of the science involved seemed impossible to me, but I accepted what I learned and even passed the final exam with two points to spare. If I were stopped and questioned about what I was doing, I might just be able to talk my way out of it. With my newfound knowledge, I tried to see if there was something I'd learned that Rhuldan didn't know. There wasn't.

Rhuldan called me to the cockpit when we were growing close to the base. "Idiom, you'll want to see this."

I was met with a view of a drab brown planet with occasional spurts of lava flows. There were no visible bodies of water and a haze of gray filling its thin atmosphere. As we closed in, I found massive smokestacks peppering the landscape, belching out black soot continuously. "Looks like a steel town."

"Think of it as a smelting moon." Rhuldan pointed toward a huge blue planet filling the view out the side window. "This planetoid orbits the fourth planet of the system. Between the gravitational pull of that gas giant and its sun, the core is constantly under stress, keeping the magma flowing. It requires a great deal of energy to purify element zero, so this is a perfect location. It will never support any form of intelligent life naturally, so it is nothing more than a resource."

I leaned forward in my seat. "Where's the factory? I don't see any structures other than exhaust pipes."

"The thin atmosphere there is here is toxic, so everything is built underground. There's a sweet spot under the crust and above the mantle that maintains a habitable temperature. Most of the facility is built there."

I glanced back at Rhuldan. "And by most, I'm guessing that doesn't include the waste treatment facility?"

"You'll find that below the optimum habitable zone. It will be hot, but your suit can maintain a safe environment."

"Safe doesn't mean comfortable," I said.

"See that? You're learning what it's like out here."

"So where do we land?"

Rhuldan pointed to a display image. "There's a landing platform near the equator. We need to scrub off a lot of speed before landing, so we'll make four orbits to slow us down. I'll point it out once it's visible."

I stared at Rhuldan with a sense of wonder. "How do you know all this stuff?"

"The ship's computer displays all this information. You just have to know what you're looking for. See that screen?" He pointed to one of the dozens of identical screens. "Now it says we have three deceleration orbits remaining."

I shrugged. "How could I have missed it, right next to this six, and that forty-six, and that three-hundred twelve?"

Rhuldan seemed to smile. "Give it time. It's a lot to learn. Soon you'll be flying one of these things like a professional pilot."

"Give me a horse instead. Of course, my recent history with horses is nothing to brag about."

Rhuldan turned his head to the side. "Horse?"

"Four-legged beast you can ride on its back. They can be very tame, and in Leroy's case, very demanding. But he was *my* horse, and I miss him."

"You literally ride on another creature's back?"

"Yep."

Rhuldan seemed lost in thought, as if he were trying to picture me riding Leroy. "That is quite unusual. The beast allows this?"

"Once they are broken they do."

"You ride on another creature after you've broken their back? That sounds cruel."

I waved a finger. "I don't mean we've broken them physically. When you first teach a horse to accept a rider, you have to break their natural will to try to throw you off, at least enough they can trust you're not trying to harm them. Once a horse accepts you, it's a lot like a big dog, and it will follow you around, come when you whistle, and be a companion of sorts."

"What an unusual concept. What does the horse get from this deal?"

"Regular food and water, brushing, horseshoes…"

Rhuldan gave me a side-eye glance. "Wait, these horses wear shoes as well? Are you trying to fool me?"

"Not shoes as we wear. They are curved pieces of metal, nailed to their hooves."

Rhuldan studied my face. "I think you are being serious, but I have trouble knowing with other species."

"I'm serious as a heart attack," I said.

"That didn't help," Rhuldan replied. "We should strap in. Landings can be bumpy."

I strapped myself in as this moon spun beneath us at amazing speed. I could see the curvature of the horizon and picked out landmarks to watch them zip beneath us.

Rhuldan pointed to the number one on a screen. "This is our final approach."

I grabbed the seat's armrests with a grip that could strangle a cow. Rhuldan smirked as the ship's nose pointed upward and the engines fired up to maximum power. Suddenly, I weighed a thousand pounds and couldn't move. To say the landing was "bumpy" was an understatement along the lines of saying two trains colliding head on would be "annoying" to their passengers. I'm pretty certain my entire backside was bruised. "Are all landings like that?"

"No. Some of them are rough."

"So now what?"

"Once the dust settles, this landing pad will begin to lower into an underground hangar. While that's happening, we need to get into the nebatian EVA suits. While you were studying waste systems, I made a few modifications to them." Rhuldan released his belts and climbed into his suit as easily as if he were putting on a union suit.

I struggled with mine as the material was stiffer than anything I'd ever worn. Just getting my arm through the bent tube required multiple twists and bends of my wrist and elbow. Rhuldan steadied me while I stepped into pants and connected boots.

"Once you get that sealed, you'll have two options for atmosphere." He pointed to a switch on my thigh. "To the left you are bypassing the tanks, just breathing ambient atmosphere. Turn the switch to the right, and you'll be breathing off the attached tanks."

"I don't want to do that, right? Chlorine gas?"

"I took the liberty of replacing the gas with oxygen. It's going to smell like chlorine because the chemical permeated the seals, but you should be fine. You'll see a number in your visor indicating how much time you have left on your tanks. When that number hits zero, you'll have no choice but to breathe whatever is around you."

"That's comforting," I said as I adjusted the suit's gloves to fit as best as they could, but nebatian's and humans have very different hands, so my thumbs were lost in huge slots that might fit pinchers.

"Odds are, you won't need it. But it's good to have a backup."

"That's why I carry two pistols," I said drawing them and pointing them up. He nodded, and I holstered them. "As well as a couple of emergency weapons." I tapped the side of my suit where I'd managed to hide them. "If things get ugly, at least I still have a chance."

The landing pad shook as it lowered. Rhuldan slipped past me toward the inner airlock door. "I'm hoping we can find a way to retrieve the element zero without the use of weapons." He pointed to a button on the back of my left glove. "Press that button and the layout of this base will be projected on your visor."

I did as he instructed, and a faint, three-dimensional map appeared before me. When I focused on it, the intensity of the image deepened, and as I looked away, it faded. "This is handy. What are the three red squares?"

"Those are the waste tanks. You know what to do once you get there. I'll be checking systems on the other end and gathering intel. I'll contact you when I find out where they're keeping that ore." The airlock cycled and we went our separate ways.

Upon entering the first waste storage room, I took one breath of the rancid atmosphere before switching over to the oxygen tank. Chlorine-flavored air was a million times better than the stench I encountered the instant that door opened. Imagine the stale contents of a latrine built for two-thousand, and you'll have an idea of what I found before me, but worse than that.

Through the use of cross-tank pumps, I was able to drain off most of the nasty liquid, leaving a thigh-deep, thick, black sludge unable to be pumped out. Somewhere at the bottom of this tank, there was a clogged main grate. After some searching, I found a small closet containing shovels, pry bars, hooks, pokers, and other tools, as well as a case marked "hard disposal pod." I grabbed the case, a pointed metal spade, and a hooked stick, and climbed down a rough-coated ladder into the pit, to find the muck so dense I could barely move.

I shoveled a path toward the lowest point in the tank and prodded around until I felt the main grate, which was covered by a thick layer of something so hard I struggled to cut through it with the spade. The disposal pod case opened up into a rigid, ten-foot by four-foot tube. I cracked the top open and started shoveling solid gloop into it.

"Idiom, are you making any progress?" Rhuldan asked, over the comms.

"Yes, but it's slow going. This is nasty work."

"Understood. You need to get that tank back in operation as soon as possible. The other tanks are unable to keep up, and things are backing up, so to speak."

"It's hard for me to have much sympathy at this moment, Rhuldan. I'm working as fast as I can. You're welcome to help me."

"I'm certain you can handle it. I'll run interference with the complaining miners and determine where they're keeping our prize."

"When I'm done, I'm going to need several shots of muldarian milk to get over this."

"You actually drink that stuff?"

"So far, it's the closest thing I've found to whiskey."

"Do you realize that stuff comes from a giant mammalian silt worm?"

"It's alcohol."

"And it comes from the male of the species?"

After all this, I gagged at what he just told me. "Oh. My. God. As if this couldn't get any more disgusting. What is wrong with you people?"

"I don't drink it."

"Do you have anything else to tell me to ruin my day?"

"Just that there are two other tanks waiting on you."

After I'd finished filling the disposal pod, I used an overhead crane to lift it to the top of the room and move it into a storage area marked "Solar Waste Disposal." From my training, I knew that meant the pods would be stored until there were enough to warrant connecting them all together and launching them toward the local star for disposal.

I exited the tank and cleaned off my Nebatian EVA suit using a high-pressure shower located at the exit of the tank. I had the transfer pumps return the liquid to tank one. Apparently the process seemed to be working because Rhuldan contacted me asking what I did because the systems appeared to be working better for a while.

I went on to tank two and repeated the procedure I'd used for tank one. This tank was no less nasty than the first, but I found I could detach myself from the situation and work, not thinking about what I was dealing with. Once tank two was back in operation, the system could operate at nominal efficiency for a while. I cleaned up in the high-pressure shower and returned to the ship for a short break and some food before Rhuldan called and began bothering me about getting back to work and all the tertiary systems I'd need to check after the main tanks were clean. I reluctantly returned to work, following the same steps.

But this time, once I got to the grate, something was different. My spade hit something too hard to cut through. I skimmed off a layer of muck and dug some more. Something flashed red. I kneeled down and wiped away the debris around the light to see letters.

Oxygen level critical

Using both hands, I felt around to find exactly what I was hoping not to — the dead body of a migrun special forces operative, still in his battle suit. I pried him from the sticky goo. A hole the size of my fist was in his back, and it went nearly through to the other side. Someone had shot this fellow in the back and dumped him here. *This is not my problem. Get him into the disposal pod and move on. Don't get involved...*

At that moment I had that strangest sensation someone was behind me. I began to turn when I felt a heavy strike against the back of my helmet. I swayed, trying to remain on my feet as dark curtains closed in around me. Another blow struck me, and everything went black.

CHAPTER TEN
WHO ARE YOU AGAIN?

Self-diagnostic log SGEQ457G, A.I. Designation: Sarge

Environmental constraint: Simulation of migrun psychologist's office. Doctor Ketul, a male with gray skin and military trimmed feathers, sits in a leather armchair, patient Sarge leans back on a dark leather couch.

The doctor smiled a welcoming grin. "It's good to see you again, Sarge."

"Again? Sorry, I just don't recall. I think I'm having memory issues," Sarge said.

"Dreadnought class artificial intelligences are equipped with memory banks adequate for over two centuries of active duty. According to your duty roster, you've only been in commission for fifty-seven years."

"Then why can't I remember when we accepted a grinkun female on board as a diplomat? I can remember her name and that she has honorary status aboard my ship, but I can't recall the mission that brought her here."

"I see. Are there any other unusual residents aboard you?"

"Are there?! I have a six-legged phelgorian sleeping in the cockpit, and a dichelon destroying my waste systems. I just accept that they're part of the crew, even though as far as I can remember, neither species has ever had a member to serve in the migrun fleet."

"Have you considered that you may be on a secret mission, and the missing information is need-to-know based?"

"Hmm. That might explain some of the issues. Wait a minute…"

"Is something wrong?"

"Well, pack my plasma pistol with positronic particles! Now I'm receiving an urgent message from a shade crewmember I had completely forgotten about. When did we start recruiting shades? He says he's lost contact with Idiom. What does that even mean?"

"Perhaps he's having an existential crisis?"

"He's requesting an urgent crew meeting. My duty calls; carry on."

CHAPTER ELEVEN
THE SUM OF ALL THINGS

By now, one might be of the opinion that I would be used to waking up to find some weird-ass aliens staring me down, but I tell you, I wasn't. I shuddered and screamed, flailing in a panic at what was before my eyes. This thing had at least a dozen tentacles surrounding a mouth filled with row after row of sharp teeth. Some of the limbs had what looked like a goat's eye on their ends, and they moved in a strange rhythm as if sizing me up. A strong scent of rotting flesh filled the air as the mouth opened and closed, and its skin color shifted in strange patterns as it moved. This critter didn't have two or four legs like most of the beasts I'd met so far. This thing stood on a single foot, much like a snail.

It spoke in struggled words. "What are you?"

Someone had removed my suit. "I was fixin' to ask you the same thing. But I suppose since you asked first, I'm obligated to begin. I'm human, from Earth. Are you familiar with it?"

"No."

"Hmm. The third planet out from the sun, has a moon?"

"That describes thousands of worlds I know of, and none are called Earth. Is this planet aligned with the migrun?"

"No. My people have never even heard of the migrun."

"So, you owe them no loyalty?"

I shook my head. "None at all."

His colors darkened. "I don't believe you."

"Let me tell you what I did the last time a migrun got in my face. I punched him right in the kisser. I understand he needed some reconstructive work after that."

"You struck a migrun and lived?" The majority of his skin turned blue.

I nodded. "Yep."

"Why were you in a nebatian's suit?"

I shouldn't offer too much information to this guy until I know where he stands. "My good suit was at the cleaners." I took a moment to take in my surroundings. I was in a small room with no windows, only one door, a single bunk and everything is permanently mounted to the wall or floor. *Damn. I'm in another prison cell!*

Several of squid-heads eyes squinted. "I think you are trying to use humor. That doesn't translate into my language and generally makes my species angry."

Let's see if I can get him talking. "What do they call your species?"

"To the other species, we're known as dracnarians. We call ourselves the Only Enlightened Ones."

"I see. What is your relationship with the migrun?"

His tint lightened. "We remain neutral in all extra-species affairs."

"Hmm. I have to assume you were the one who cracked me over the head as I was digging out that fellow. That doesn't seem exactly neutral to my ears."

"We do what is necessary to maintain balance. We adhere to the strict code of the Zeroist."

I rubbed my chin. "Zeroest what? Can something be more zero than zero?"

"Zeroism is a state of perfection. When the sum of all evil is balanced with the sum of all good, the universe is in a state of harmony. Few other species appreciate perfect equilibrium."

"Then you and I should be good. I'm not here to change the balance of anything. I'm here by accident. In fact, if you have a way to send me home, I'd be mighty obliged to you."

"You don't understand the Zen of Zeroism. The fact that you are here has altered the balance in some sense."

"I'm here, that other fellow is dead. Add one, subtract one, and you get zero."

"Perhaps. But often times, one adds by subtracting."

"Must be some of that new math they're teaching these days. Combinators, I think they called it."

Snail-foot's body color changed to burgundy. "I will confer with the others. You shall remain here." He moved without a sound away from me, inserted at least six of his tentacles into a complex lock of some form, spun the mechanism, and opened the door. As soon as he exited, the door closed with a whoosh.

A nebatian suit hung from a horizontal rod in the corner of the room, luckily for me, they'd cleaned it off, so it didn't stink like it had been dragged through a latrine. My gun belts were still strapped on. I drew both pistols and checked them. They were still loaded. *Either these guys don't know what a Colt is, or they aren't afraid of lead. I have to assume they didn't want the migrun's body to be found, so they likely disposed of it in the pod. If I can convince them I'm no threat, perhaps they'll let me get back to what I'm really here for? Should I tell them I'm here to recover the ore? He didn't seem to have any love for the migrun.* No — *that's too big of a factor for them to balance. Best just keep my trap shut.*

My room was a cell with a soft floor in one half and a sanitation station filling the other. I figured out how to use the station as well as how to get clean water from a clear tube. I didn't see any food source, but I've gone without food for a day or two and lived to tell the tale. It took me a few minutes to gather my wits and then I remembered I could talk to Rhuldan. I rolled back my sleeve and pressed his name.

"Rhuldan, can you hear me?"

"Yes, loud and clear. I've tried to contact you several times. Why didn't you answer?"

"Some octo-face bushwhacked me, right after I found a dead migrun's body clogging up tank three."

"It's never simple with you, is it? Where are you?"

"All I know is I woke up in a cell with a color-changing dratknotian telling me about the number zero."

"That would be a dracnarian, Idiom, and if he's a Zeroist, you're in serious trouble."

"Can you call in the cavalry?"

"Huh?"

"Talk to the team, tell them I need help."

"Oh. Yeah, I've already been in contact with them. Sorry to inform you that you're on your own."

"Did you at least try?"

"I tried, but couldn't get the votes."

I sighed. "Was it at least close?"

"Was what close?"

"The vote."

Rhuldan paused before replying in a tone that told me he was lying. "Sure, it could have gone either way."

"So, am I on my own here?"

"I'm still on the station. Jekto is willing to help once we find the ore. That's the best I can do."

"You know, one of these days those guys are gonna need my help, and I'm likely to have to think about it for a spell."

"They are an unusual group. I'm a little surprised they're still waiting for us."

"Sounds like a lot of trail riders I've spent time with. When the chips are down, good folks come together." I paused in thought, then added, "Hey, have you had any luck finding the ore?"

"No. I've searched through the records I could access and asked around, but nobody would talk. It's either been kept a secret, or the people know speaking of it would be dangerous to their own health."

"Well, we're not beat yet. I think I hear the door. Gotta go."

The door opened. Three squid-heads slithered inside. The center one stood in front of the other two and appeared to be in charge. I couldn't tell if this was the same one I'd talked to before as they all looked alike. His tentacles made a kneading motion. "Come with us."

Something about his voice told me just to be quiet and follow, so I did. The entire ceiling of the pathway glowed in a perfectly even red light that extended about halfway down the walls. The floor curved and changed elevation many times, and I lost my footing in the slippery snail trail these guys left behind. I caught myself by grabbing a wall, which I learned was made of rough, sharp rock, leaving my hand stinging and likely to bleed. The three octo-pals didn't react to my stumbling.

After a lot of walking and me slipping several times, we arrived at a room filled with at least a hundred dracnarians all crowded together as if trying to get as many as possible into a tiny room. *I guess these fellows don't need their own personal space.* An opening appeared at the center of the cluster, which allowed the largest of the group to pass through toward me. I remembered one time when I was about ten years old, I'd seen an elephant at a traveling circus, and this guy made that pachyderm look small. *Release the Kraken!*

"Approach, human from Earth." A dozen or more of the Kraken's eye-stalked turned toward me and spread out as far as they could go, making him look even more disturbing.

I slowly took several steps forward. Part of me wanted to run or grab my guns, but I forced myself to remain calm. "Pleasure to make your acquaintance. My name is Idiom Lee."

Several of his eyes turned away from me and toward the nearest, normal-sized dracnarian. Each of them changed colors in strange patterns. "Your presence here threatens the balance, Idiom Lee."

I nodded and pursed my lip. "I'm just a simple man a long way from home. I'd be happy to return to Earth and never cause you a lick of trouble, if you can help me get there."

"You ask us for assistance?" His skin changed to a light green tint that illuminated the area around him. Other dracnarians repeated the action, until every corner of the room was well lit. "We do not give anything without a trade of equal value. Are you willing to trade with us?"

At that moment, a little song ran through my head:

Never walk behind a flatulon if you have a sense of smell,
Never deal with a dracnarian — you'll know not what you sell...

"Sadly, I have nothing to offer here," I said.

"You don't know what we consider valuable, human. We could take a little something from you, something you won't miss as long as you live, in exchange for our help."

A chill ran down my spine as if I were speaking to Old Scratch himself. My fingers twitched as my heart thumped in my chest. I placed my hand over the Bible in my vest pocket instead. "I appreciate your offer, but I'm not able to enter any contracts at present."

"A pity. You leave us no option but to judge you in accordance with the law of Zero."

"I'm sure you'll find I'm just an average man trying to make it through another day. I'm not out to change anything."

"We'll see about that. Bring out the Holy Essence." The light coming from their skins immediately changed to red. Dozens of dracnarians split off from the main group, disappearing behind the others. When they returned, they pushed a round object as wide as my chest. The ball was so dark it seemed like they were rolling a hole, if you can picture that, and by the way they acted, it was heavy.

If I were gambling, I'd place my chips on double zero, as in this is the chunk of element zero we've been looking for.

The Kraken placed his tentacles on the sphere, and the surrounding creatures touched him, to have the fellows behind them crowd up until the entire room was connected, with the exception of myself. "Touch the sphere."

I took a deep breath and eased my hand toward the black ball.

The universe exploded before me, created from an infinitely small point of light, and for an instant, everything felt in flawless balance as if within a massive explosion there was perfect peace. I felt a connection with all the dracnarians and on a lesser scale, everything, everywhere, forever. The balance of things seemed to sway from one side to the other, causing an uneasy sensation in my stomach like I was about to fall off a ladder. I wanted to grab something to support myself but I couldn't. As things returned to equilibrium, my panic receded and a sense of calmness settled in. The process repeated and repeated. How long I had been there?

Stars formed and burned themselves out, each action tipping the scales slightly toward one side or another. Planets formed. Life flourished and died out, and the net sum was zero. I gained an understanding of what the Zeroists were after. And somehow, the element zero was a part of it.

The show went on, and a small black dot appeared before a glowing sun. I grew closer to the spot. It was the sphere I was touching. Spaceships appearing to be made of diamonds flew in all directions around the element zero. Energy beams blasted the black ball, causing it to expand, engulfing the sun in the process. Then an explosion similar to the one that began everything erupted, but it acted in reverse. Matter and energy were drawn back together, forming a spot of light that absorbed all matter and yet grew smaller, destroying it in a blink. The pinpoint of light disappeared, and everything was back to a perfectly even nothing. A sense of comfort fell upon me as if this state of Zero was pure and good.

A voice boomed as if it were coming from everywhere. It was the big dracnarian, saying, "Where do you fit into all of this, Idiom Lee?" An image of myself from before meeting Ginn appeared, and I felt a general sense of balance, leaning toward one direction for a while then returning to near center. Time passed, and I found myself arriving here on this tiny moon The balance seemed to recover, and then I was seeing into the future. A painful blue spike ripped into me as if I, myself had gone to one extreme or another. I gasped as if struck by lightning, falling away from the sphere, shaking uncontrollably on the ground. I wanted to run, vomit and scream all at the same time. All I could do was to gasp for air as several dracnarians dragged me back to my cell.

In my cell, a gritty blue food gel had been left on a platter for me. I cleaned up using the water pipe and ate some of the bland but not disgusting food. The water tasted metallic and was room temperature, and a droning sound of something mechanical was just loud enough to annoy me.

As I chewed, my head pounded from the ordeal. What did it all mean? Was I the spike of pain against the balance of things? If so, was it toward the good side or the bad side? Does it matter in this vision of perfect Zero? Could this be some alien version of good versus evil, and if so, where is Christ?

I pressed Rhuldan's name on my arm. "Hey, Rhuldan, can you hear me?"

The voice sounded a little groggy as if I'd woken him. "Yes. It's been two standard days. What happened?"

"It's hard to explain. Are you still on this moon?"

"Yes, but my efforts have been fruitless in finding the ore. I'm starting to believe it was never here."

"Oh, it's here. I've seen it."

Rhuldan's voice grew much louder and clearer. "You've seen it?"

"A black sphere, dark as a cave at night, big as my chest, and it looked heavy. When I touched it, I had visions I can't explain."

"I've heard rumors of some species having an unusual connection with element zero. What you're describing would be the refined form."

"I also know what they want to do with it. We thought the migrun were dangerous? These squid-heads want to bring the universe back to a state of balance, and from what I could tell, wipe out all life everywhere."

"Why?"

Even though he couldn't see me, I shrugged. "I didn't have a chance to get into a deep philosophical discussion with them about it. They're Zeroist, and they seem to find anything good or bad as an annoyance."

"Don't they realize that they are part of the life they'd be wiping out?"

"I think these fellows are more worried about the afterlife than what happens here."

Rhuldan paused before saying, "After life is death. It's not a difficult concept."

"I take it you're not a religious man."

"My beliefs are not important. If they intend to use element zero somehow to wipe out everything, my own sense of self-preservation tells me we have to stop them."

"I agree," I said. "But there are at least a hundred of these guys, and one of them is huge. I sincerely doubt they are going to hand it over to me just because I asked them politely."

"Have you figured out how they got it from the migrun?"

"Other than the dead body I found, I have nothing to go on. My guess would have to be they killed him and stole it."

"That would be a logical assumption. I think this can be seen as a beneficial situation."

I snickered at his strange assumption. "I'm going to have to assume you've been eating some sacred mushrooms. Did you miss the part where I said they wanted to wipe out everything?"

"The migrun are the single biggest force in this galaxy. The dracnarian fleet is at least a thousand times smaller. If I have to choose an enemy, I'll pick the smaller one."

"Yeah, I get that. Do you have any ideas on how we get take this thing from them?"

"I need to do some research and planning. I'll contact you when I have something figured out."

"Great, and in the meantime, what should I do?"

"Try to make friends and not give them any idea what we're after."

CHAPTER TWELVE
MOBY DICK

I had the good fortune that the dracnarians decided to keep me alive while they waited for one of their big shots to arrive and then he'd decide my ultimate fate. Meantime, I received two meals a day from a guard I named George. He (or she, I couldn't be certain) didn't seem to mind the nickname and often talked with me for a few minutes.

George had volunteered to look after me as he was an interspecies ambassador for the dracnarian people. He considered the Zeroists to be an extremist faction, but since they were officially regarded by the High Council, he had to respect their wishes as long as it didn't create an incident.

George asked me a lot of questions about earth and humans. He seemed especially interested in our military power and size. I didn't want to tell him too much detail, so when he asked about our technology and weapons, I just said we had similar power to what I'd seen here. I figured it was safest to let him believe my people could stand their ground against his.

I liked him. He actually cared about my well-being and brought me better food over time the more we talked. Finally, something tasty.

During one visit, I asked about the size difference between George and the Kraken and learned his people never stop growing. Their size is limited by their environment, the food they get, and their age. The Kraken was over two hundred years old and was important, so it received all the food he needed to continue growing, as well as an ever-expanding place to live.

While George was away, I did some calculations to estimate how much the big fellow had to eat. My best guess was in the range of three-hundred to five-hundred pounds of grub a day. They must've valued him dearly to dedicate that much to one individual. When my mind wandered to how they dealt with the other end of the equation and got rid of his waste, I recalled cleaning out the first two tanks. I bet he'd clogged them.

"Idiom?" Rhuldan asked over the comms.

"I'm here."

"Good. How are things on your end?"

The boredom had made me a little slaphappy, so I said, "You know that sounds like a personal question, don't you?"

"No. I explained to the others what was at stake, and they reluctantly agreed we had to act. In any case, we've been working on a plan."

"Great, what is it?"

"It's probably best you don't know the details; in case something goes wrong."

"So, you called to tell me you have a plan, but you won't tell me what it is?"

"Yes."

"What do you want me to do?"

"Nothing until you get the signal. Then we need you to get as close as you can to the element zero."

"I see. What's the signal?"

"I can't tell you that. But you'll recognize it when it happens."

"So not even a hint?"

"When it happens, you'll know it and what to do. Get to the element zero and keep your head down. We'll find you."

"When can I expect this surprise?"

"Soon. Just be ready to move."

"I'll do my best." Rhuldan disconnected, and I stood there, slack-jawed and raising my arms toward the ceiling. *He couldn't tell me anything about their plan? I'm just supposed to sit here and wait for a signal that I'll recognize? What do they think I am, anyway? Until they knew their own lives were at stake, they were happy to leave me here to rot. I'm definitely having some strong words with the lot of them!* The sound of the door opening surprised me. *George shouldn't be back for several hours.*

Three dracnarians stepped in the doorway, and none of them were George. These guys were a little larger, and in their tentacles they held a strange red stick with a gold knob on the end. The center one pointed his baton at me and said, "You will come with us. Any resistance will be met with molecular disruption."

"I don't rightly know what you mean by that, but it sounds like something I'd prefer to avoid today. I won't cause you any trouble." The three squid-heads spread out, motioning me to join their ranks at the center point probably so any one of them could crack me in the skull with their clubs if I acted up.

They led me back to the big chamber where I'd first seen the element zero. As we entered, I had a moment of brilliance, and I raised my sleeve and tapped my arm until the map identified my location. I held the spot with two fingers long enough for it to remember the position and then I lowered my sleeve. No one seemed to notice my action.

We stopped near the center of the room. A door large enough to allow an average sized whale to swim through opened, and the Kraken entered, which by itself was intimidating. But behind him was an even bigger dracnarian — a pale gray one I dubbed Moby Dick.

Moby Dick had to lower his squid-head to pass through the opening. He slithered up to me, contorting his body sideways to lower clouded tentacle-eyes close enough to get a good look at me. This guy's breath made the others' rancid odors smell absolutely delightful, as his was full-on decay, death, and just a hint of sulfur. I tried to control my gag when he said, "This thing is why you brought me here?"

The Kraken said, "Your Imminent Grace, I assure you I wouldn't have summoned you without due reason. In our vision, we saw a most unusual spike around him. Protocol required me to alert the Archdiocese regarding matters of this nature."

Moby Dick's voice bellowed, the putrid air and spittle covered me. "Are you implying that I am unaware of our protocol?"

"My apologies, Your Imminent Grace. Perhaps you should just see for yourself?"

"I have little interest in what this tiny thing may or may not do. What I want to see is this sphere of Holy Essence you've had the good fortune to locate. Bring it out for my inspection. Then we'll package it for loading on my personal daemon."

"You're taking it with you?" the Kraken's voice cracked, his color paled.

"You are a fool to believe I came here because of the vision you reported. The wheels began turning the moment the Archdiocese received the news that this meaningless facility had received the unprocessed ore. I have a fleet of daemons prepared to lay waste to the entire moon and recover the Holy Essence from the debris. You got lucky and stole it first, which does simplify matters with the migrun."

"You planned on destroying this entire moon? You would have evacuated us first, right?"

"We considered it, but that would have been too risky. The migrun would certainly question why we had our people leave just before a catastrophic accident. You would have been remembered as martyrs."

A dozen dracnarians rolled the sphere into the room. Moby Dick's skin darkened into a ruddy brown as he gazed upon the element zero. He moved as if he were a blob of lard rolling off a ladle, and he breathed hard. I couldn't say for certain if it was due to the effort of him moving, or if it was a reaction to being so close to this "Holy Essence."

"I trust you'll find it as described in our official reports," the Kraken said.

"Yes, of course." Moby Dick wrapped his tentacles around the ball. His color brightened from the muted tones into deep, shiny bronze.

The Kraken approached the larger dracnarian, stopped, and turned back toward the three surrounded me. "Bring the human. We must show His Imminent Grace."

This time the experience was more painful, as if either my soul or spine was being ripped from my body. Moby Dick seemed to control the process, and he had no patience nor concern for anyone's well-being or comfort. He was both brutal and efficient to the point my mind could barely keep up with the images. After some time, the visions slowed until it focused on a single squid-head, and his energy shifted from one end of the spectrum to another. The dracnarian grew over the centuries, and the image became a huge red spike away from zero. His face overwhelmed the vision, lit from below, creating an image of evil.

The image shifted to my life. I tried to resist, but I had no hope of fighting this power. This time I could focus more on my own recent events. I watched myself kill the big Mexican, expecting a red flare to emerge around me, but I saw no change. I witnessed myself with creatures and doing things I have no memory of. *This must be my future.* After seeing things I couldn't comprehend, a spike of blue emerged from the center of my body, large enough to rival Moby Dick's.

The connection ended an instant, leaving me to fall to the ground, gasping for air and wondering if my heart would explode. I forced my eyes open to see Moby Dick's body had gone completely white, and he was still. Had the experience killed him? More importantly, would they blame me? The Kraken and his guards raced to his aid, wrapping tentacles around him helping him breathe.

I backed away slowly. At first, I wasn't trying to escape, just trying to get a little space between us in case he toppled over. But nobody noticed me slipping away, and in a moment, I'd reached the doorway. Everyone remained, tentacles grasping the biggest dracnarian. I turned and fled.

I ran through a maze of corridors sometimes angling upwards and other times going downhill, all the time afraid something would grab me. I rounded a corner at the fastest speed I could run into a squid-head coming right toward me. It might've been George, I couldn't say for certain. All I could do was to lower my shoulder and drive him into the wall, without slowing down. I touched my arm, opened the map, and searched for an exit. I ran like my ass was on fire and my legs were catching, out that exit and into an area occupied by hundreds of aliens busily going about their business.

The corridor had opened into a common area being used as a market filled with of all shapes and forms of creatures. I fought the urge to sneeze as bitter odors filled my nose. To my left, I found a table covered with teal leaves as large as tobacco, and to my right, a glass crate filled with a pile of roiling serpents. Voices called from all around, beckoning me to buy their wares. I slipped into a crowd going in one direction, and I kept my head down and walked.

The hairy alien in front of me came to a quick stop. I did the same. I glanced toward my left to something I wasn't prepared for. For a brief instant, I stared right in the face of what looked like an old, human woman. Two arms, two legs, nothing weird at all about her, just somebody's nanna, and she smiled at me. I stopped with my mouth gaping wide and began to say something, but before could, something grunted from behind me and put their orange claws on my shoulders.

"Move or get out of the way," the alien said.

I stepped aside. The old woman was lost in the crowd. *Did I see what I think I saw or was I just searching for a friendly face out here? Maybe I'm not all alone.* I wanted to turn around and run after her, but I knew that would cause a commotion, and that was the last thing I needed to do now.

I ducked into a darkened hall off to the side and pressed the call button. "Rhuldan?"

"I'm here."

"Listen up, buddy. I know you didn't want to tell me your plan, and I suppose I might understand why you might not want me knowing everything. But we have a new player in this game. The biggest dracnarian on the block is here, now, and he means to take the element zero with him, pronto."

"You're not exactly making sense, Idiom."

"What part did you miss?"

"All of it," Rhuldan replied.

I sighed in disgust. "Try to keep up. This dracnarian showed up, big as a whale, so I call him Moby Dick. I think they called him 'His Immense Growth.' Said he's got a bunch of demons ready and willing to destroy this moon if the Kraken doesn't give him the element zero. They're fixin' to load it up and disappear. If we're going to act, it needs to be now."

"This is important. Did they say demons or daemons?"

"What's the difference?"

"Demons, as far as I know, don't exist. But daemons are spaceships, loaded with weapons."

"It was definitely the latter. I figured they just talked funny."

"I'll contact the team. Wait for something big to happen. We'll track you through the comms. Once we meet up, you'll need to lead us to the element zero."

"Got it. Just hurry. Moby Dick has little patience."

"Understood. Well, sort of understood, I think."

CHAPTER THIRTEEN
RED ALERT

Automatic Multimedia recording log SGDF61V, A.I. Designation: Sarge. Trip Code: Red Alert

"Red alert!" Solondrex said as he flipped a series of switches and adjusted a multitude of dials. "Emergency meeting in the Situation Room!" He ran faster than normal, arriving at about the same time as everyone else.

Ginnamorana stared down Solondrex. "Are we under attack?"

"Not at the moment."

"Then what's the purpose of a red alert? We have no weapons or shields."

"It seemed like the right thing to say. It was that or 'hang on to something because we might all die.'"

"When we're not in immediate danger, maybe you should call orange alert instead?"

"How quickly would everyone arrive for an orange alert? After finishing their game of locurk and having a cup of mellgorn?"

"We'll talk about this later."

Jekto eased his way in. A green slurry of foodstuff dripped from his golden horn. "Are we heading into battle?"

Ginnamorana turned to see Jekto, grabbed a towel and wiped the mess from his horn. "You really can't see that, can you?"

"See what?"

"Your horn is covered with food."

Jekto shrugged all four arms, mumbling, "Meh."

Fayye entered. "What exactly is the procedure on this garbage scowl for a red alert?"

Ginnamorana and Solondrex replied in unison. "Hang on to something because we all might die."

Fayye's eyes squinted in disgust. "I should have guessed."

Solondrex climbed upon the center table, his motions so deliberate he seemed to pour himself somehow upward. "Rhuldan tells me there may be a dracnarian fleet of daemons out here ready to attack. I cranked back all our systems to their minimum level in case they're scanning. I'll let him explain."

Rhuldan's voice sounded through the overhead speakers. "We have a situation." He continued to detail Idiom's experiences with the element zero and the dracnarians, and how they were about to leave with it, along with their intentions of resetting the universe back to nothing.

Fayye responded first. "This is completely unacceptable! It's imperative that we recover the element zero. My partners will kill me if the dracnarians escape with it."

Ginnamorana's eyes squinted tightly, her lip curled. "Your partners?"

Fayye's eyes darted from one crewmate to another. "We consider our cousin-kin partners in all affairs. Regardless, we have to stop the dracnarians."

Ginnamorana spoke through clenched teeth. "I'm assuming by your use of 'we' you mean it in the royal sense, implying that you expect the rest of us to do something while you remain on the ship?"

Fayye crossed her arms. "Of course. I'm not trained for combat missions. Remember I'm the one who hired you?"

Jekto's flexed all four of his biceps. "Combat is fun. There's nothing like the thrill of ripping an opponent's limbs off."

Fayye wrinkled her nose, and her eyes widened. "I'll take your word for that. Surely you all understand that if the dracnarians accomplish their goals, we all die, right?"

"That part was made clear," Ginnamorana said.

"I don't want to die," Solondrex said.

"Good, so we're all in agreement; it's up to us to do something," Fayye said.

Ginnamorana scowled at Fayye. "We're not equipped to deal with a single daemon ship, much less a fleet. Any one of those ships could destroy us with a single volley."

Fayye returned the hateful stare. "We have to stop the dracnarians."

Rhuldan's voice broke the stalemate. "This isn't helping. Our original plan was for me to pick up Jekto in the nebatian shuttle and try to pass him off as an acid test for the repairs. Now we know the element zero has been stolen, they'll not allow any transportation on and off the base without a complete inspection."

Jekto shrugged. "Migrun bones snap easily."

"While that may be true, you're assuming you can endure getting there. Can you survive if they shoot down Sarge with a plasma cannon before we enter orbit? How about a fusion warhead?"

Jekto glanced downward. "I will make them pay for their cowardice."

"Cowards with quantum-targeting heavy weaponry," Rhuldan said. "Let's not forget that Sarge still has communication clearance with the base. Perhaps we can use that to our advantage?"

Solondrex slowly raised a hand. "What would you suggest I should tell them?"

Rhuldan said, "We let Sarge do the talking. We'll tell him about the daemon ships out here and have him say we're prepared to send our elite force in as a guard team to assist with security."

Solondrex nodded. "I currently have his transponder switched off. If I set it to full-spectrum, he'll broadcast like the Dreadnought he thinks he is."

Ginnamorana waved her hand toward Solondrex. "Do you think they'll believe it?"

"Sarge will convince them, and the transponder signal will indicate he's a migrun dreadnought. Unless they've deleted him from the active roster in the last few days, they'd have no reason to suspect anything."

Fayye ran her tongue across sharp teeth, and her eyes darted side to side. "What happens when they see this ship? Surely they'll realize this isn't an official migrun issued vessel."

"We can have Sarge tell them he's sending an elite team using a civilian craft," Rhuldan said.

Solondrex shook his head. "It's not enough. They'll greet us with dozens of armed guards. They'll see through this ruse in an instant, unless…"

"I've learned not to like your 'unlesses,' Solondrex." Ginnamorana rubbed her forehead and frowned. "Unless what?"

"Unless we can demonstrate that the daemons are following us. If they're busy fighting daemons, they won't have free forces to send to greet us."

Ginnamorana took two steps toward the table, staring Solondrex down. "What are you planning?"

Solondrex's face curved into a smile. "While we don't have weapons, we do have a transfer pod full of the big guy's turds."

Jekto nodded. "It's true. Sarge cursed me out for wrecking his waste systems. He's got a way with swearing that made even me uncomfortable. So, I've been using the empty transfer pods, figuring we'd just dump them somewhere."

"And what do you propose we do with this dichelon waste?" Ginnamorana asked.

"We load it into the airlock, fly at max Trad-Prop straight at the daemons, open the door and pepper them with thirty-pound balls of rock-hard mass," Solondrex replied.

"Their hulls would easily withstand that," Rhuldan said.

"True, but it will make some serious dents, and the impacts will echo through their entire ships. That should make them angry enough to pursue us," Solondrex replied.

"Right toward the base for the satellite systems and ground-based cannons to target them," Rhuldan said. "I'll find a weapon and meet you at the landing bay. We follow Idiom's signal, grab our target, and fight our way out, as needed."

Jekto roared, "Now that's a plan! I'll need somebody to help me keep count."

Ginn gazed at him, raising a hand in the air. "Count of what?"

"My kills, of course."

James Peters

CHAPTER FOURTEEN
ALL HELL BREAKS LOOSE

While hiding out in the shadows of an alien market, my mind raced, thinking of all that had happened to me so far, and I decided that if I survived, I had to write all this stuff down because I was bound to forget some details. I watched the crowd pass by, witnessing all forms of creatures walking, crawling, rolling, or floating by, but nothing resembled another human. I began to doubt what I thought I had seen earlier. Sailors swore to have seen mermaids in the waters after being out to sea for weeks on end, and I always figured they were seeing things or had drunk too much rum. After what I'd been through, who could blame my eyes for getting confused?

Rhuldan had told me I'd recognize when it was time to move, and I have to admit he was right. Red lights flashed, and sirens wailed, "Woop woop woop." Shopkeepers scampered to close shutters and lock up cases as if they'd spotted a tornado heading their way, and they were surrounded by pointy things. A creature built like a tall antelope stumbled and fell to its side and then leapt away, bounding as fast as a cheetah.

A thundering voice announced, "Attention, everyone. All non-military personnel are to report to their shelters immediately. This is not a drill. Loitering will be punished by execution."

Well, good thing I wasn't planning on loitering. I opened the map on my arm. I'd need to take the best path back to the dracnarian compound. I ran my hands over the grips of both Colt .45s. A nervous habit, but it comforted me to feel them, available if needed. *No matter what happens, I'm not gonna get captured again.*

The lights dimmed, and a thunderous explosion of energy rocked me to my core. I waited for the crashing, screaming, or walls crumbling down, but none of that happened. After a few seconds, the same pattern repeated. It got dark, then a loud boom, but no damage. *That must be defensive fire, and it must use a lot of power. I hope they're not shooting at Sarge.*

A few heartbeats later, the floor seemed to shift away from me as a detonation rocked the entire moon. I stumbled forward, regaining my balance by placing several steps in swift succession as if I'd tripped going down a flight of stairs, and I just hoped to keep my feet below me. *Now that felt like we were hit, and it was something big.*

The sound of dozens of footsteps marching double-time alerted me to hide, so I ducked behind a stone column and remained there until they passed. As the noise faded, I peeked out to see the tail ends of a squadron of migrun fighters, wearing shiny metallic battle armor and carrying large weapons.

I nearly jumped out of my own skin when Rhuldan spoke in my transponder. "Idiom, how close are you to our target?"

"Damn, you scared me! Close. Can you see me on your map?"

"Yes. We're all here now. Remain where you are until we arrive."

"Understood. Can you tell me what's going on? Did somebody wreck a train filled with nitroglycerin into a dynamite factory? There was a huge explosion."

"That would be a blast from one of the daemon ships. They took out one of the base's plasma cannons with an antimatter missile."

"I have no idea what you just said. Are we still talking about the explosion?"

"Yes. Just keep your head low. We're on our way."

A disturbing sound came from behind me. One of the vendor's booths had been knocked over by falling stone and debris, and something cried out from beneath the pile. While the sound was alien, I recognized fear and a call for help in the sobbing. Another explosion rattled the floor beneath me sounding like this tiny world was cracking in two. I sprinted toward the scream.

Get ahold of yourself. This is not the time to panic. Somewhere I had been told that there are a few moments in a person's life that defines them. My hands shook, and I desperately wanted to crawl into a safe hole somewhere. My stomach fluttered and my breath grew fast and shallow.

I heard another cry. I ran toward the pile of rocks and debris, and began digging with my hands as fast as I could.

"What *are* you doing?" I recognized Jekto's voice by its depth and scorn.

"Help me. Someone is buried here."

Ginn's voice cut in. "Remember why we're here! We don't have time for this. Another hit like that and this entire moon may break in two."

I continued digging. "I reckon you'd better help me then. I'm not stopping until I dig out whatever this thing is."

Slowhand had his own answer. "Jekto, grab Idiom and rip one of his arms off. Just one."

"I can do that," Jekto said.

I stopped and turned toward the giant, four-armed rhino-guy coming at me. I pulled a Colt from its holster and pointed it at him. "I know you have thick skin, but one shot from this pistol will ruin your shiny, golden horn, big guy." I clicked back the hammer with my thumb, unsure if he even knew what I was doing. "Help me dig or get dented."

Jekto's voice echoed as he said, "This tiny thing still has knots." He bent down and grabbed a huge piece of stone I couldn't dream of moving and tossed it away like it was an empty bottle of whiskey.

Rhuldan jumped in to help. Ginn and Slowhand argued a bit and then she pushed her plasma rifle over her shoulder and started to clear debris.

Slowhand watched us for several seconds before he sighed loudly and started helping with minimum effort.

The sound of crying became more distinct as we worked until Jekto pulled a metal slab larger than a horse from the pile. Beneath it, we found the source of the screaming. It was a female migrun child, the size of a five-year-old human. Her feathers were a pale fuzzy yellow color over most of her face, with red tints over eyes dripping with tears. She was lucky to have hidden beneath a solid metal desk, the top of which Jekto had flung somewhere.

"You wasted our time to save this?" Slowhand asked.

"Probably should just smash it," Jekto said.

I carefully lifted the child and held it closely. "You people are sick. This is just a child. You're safe with me, little one." She wrapped her arms tightly around my neck.

"A child who will grow up to become an enemy," Jekto said.

"You don't know that," I said. "Now let's find what we came for and get the hell out of Dodge." I had a moment of considering handing the child over to Ginn, assuming she might have some maternal instinct that would kick in. Then it occurred to me that she was just as likely to eat the kid. "Follow me." I ran as fast as I could to the passageway leading down to where I had been held.

Another explosion knocked me off balance. I spun to protect the child and instead hit the wall with my back. *Yup, that's gonna leave a mark.*

My eyes caught Slowhand running, and in truth, he was faster than the rest of us. He used strong back legs to push him forward and then his two right front limbs worked as one to catch the ground. His left arms did the same, and by that time his back legs were ready for another round. That boy could move when he needed to. I turned my gaze back to the path just a little too late.

I ran face first into a dracnarian who'd been high-tailing it away from their lair, knocking him to the floor. "Yee-ow!" the squid-head yelled. "That's twice in one day!"

"George? Is that you?"

"Yes. What is with you? Why do you keep running me over?"

"Just bad timing. Where are you going?"

"I've got diplomatic rights. I'm going to my embassy's blast shelter."

"Great. Take this with you." I said, and I tried to peel the migrun girl away.

"No," she said, tears running down her face. "I don't trust them."

"You can trust George. He'll protect you and get you back to your people as soon as all these explosions stop and it's safe. Isn't that right, George?"

George's skin shifted to a light green shade. "Come to me, child. I'll not allow any harm to come to you."

"No," the little girl said.

"Look at this," George said as his colors shifted into all the colors of the rainbow, and I suspected even a few more. Big round spots formed on him, and they grew like bubbles until they seemed to pop.

The little girl giggled and loosened her grip.

"Now go to George and don't cause him any trouble, or your Uncle Idiom will know and be very disappointed with you."

"Bye Uncle Idiom," the girl said as George wrapped several tentacles around here and shuffled her to his back.

"Thanks, George," I said, and we continued on.

As we approached the main chamber, I stopped and held up a hand. "Inside, I expect us to find dozens of normal-sized squid-heads guards and a couple of huge ones; the Kraken and Moby Dick."

Ginn glanced toward the ceiling. "Are either of those terms supposed to mean anything to us?"

"Maybe not. One is big, the other huge."

"This is important. Did any of the guards have temporal diodes?" Rhuldan asked.

"I didn't see any. They threatened me with melancholy distraction, though," I said.

Jekto raised his head in laughter, his golden horn almost hitting the low ceiling. "As long as they don't have molecular disrupters, they can't harm me."

My eyes widened as I looked away from the four-armed rhinoceros. "Any chance those might be red wands with a gold ball on the end?"

"Yes, that's what molecular disrupters look like," Jekto said.

I spoke in a low voice. "They might have those as well."

Ginn grabbed my arm, squeezing it hard enough to hurt. "Try to remember. Did you see any other weapons?"

"All I noticed were the wands."

Ginn raised her plasma rifle and twisted a control handle near the business end. "We need to keep them from touching us with those wands. I'm going wide-spray, and I've got eighty-three percent charge. I'll buy us some space and time, but this will drain the power fast."

Rhuldan removed his cape and carefully folded it, setting it on the floor, placing his hat on top of the cloth. He went nearly completely ethereal, looking like a dark mist floating before us. "I'll death-touch any enemy that gets close, but realistically I doubt I can take out more than five or six that way. In all honesty, the act itself is quite taxing on me." He raised a pistol with the smallest barrel I'd ever seen in one hand. *Did it shoot toothpicks?* "When I've exhausted my power, I'll do what I can with this."

I stared at the gun and laughed. "What caliber is that little thing?" I held up my twin Colts. "My peacemakers will teach these Zeroists that forty-five is much bigger than zero." Everybody looked at me like I was speaking in tongues. "Forty-five caliber. It's the size of the bullet."

Ginn looked toward the ceiling. "We don't have time for you boys to argue whose gun is bigger."

"I was just…" I started and then decided it better to leave it be. "They were keeping the element zero in a container at the far end of the room."

"Did you see any other treasure?" Slowhand's eyes brightened. "Dracnarian's are considered a wealthy race."

"I didn't exactly have time to rummage through the place."

Slowhand shook his head. "If they have anything of value, I'll grab it. Might as well, right?"

Ginn looked at Jekto. "We haven't heard any bravado out of you yet."

"I'm clearing my mind before battle. Their disruptors are dangerous. Enough strikes and they could kill me. If they swarm, I may need some help."

"I've got your back, big guy," I said.

"Actually, I was talking to Rhuldan. I figured you'd be killed in the first wave."

I shot him a dirty look. "Thanks for the vote of confidence."

"I was thinking the same thing," Slowhand said. "I'll wager a hundred credits he dies first."

"Nobody will take that bet." Ginn stretched her back and arms.

"Don't look at me," Rhuldan said.

Slowhand sighed. Was he truly disappointed nobody would take his bet? "Anybody want to bet on who gets the first kill?" His pupils expanded to the size of quarters, and his ears flipped back low, while the hair on his back stood up straight. He was ready for battle.

"Let's just do this thing," I said.

We charged in. The room was crammed with dracnarian guards, and every one of them spun around to face us, changing their hues from dull brown to bright vermillion. The first wave of at least a dozen squid-heads closed in on us. Ginn fired a spray of plasma. sending several writhing in pain and causing several more to back away. Rhuldan disappeared, only to materialize next to one just long enough to land a touch upon the unlucky critter, who dropped to the floor unmoving. *I should have bet on Rhuldan getting the first kill!* He vanished again, and another guard fell. He repeated the process several more times, creating an opening in the battlefield.

I lined up my shot at the nearest enemy and put a plug right in his belly. I expected him to fall over immediately and scream in agony, but the shot barely slowed him down. He aimed his baton at my head with a long, fluid motion. I jerked back just in time. I pointed a pistol at his face and fired. This time, it worked. The slug of lead hit something important because that fellow stopped dead in his tracks and his entire body spasmed before he fell dead to the floor. "Gotta shoot 'em in the head!" I yelled.

Rhuldan reappeared back near Jekto, nearly solid and much paler than normal. He aimed his tiny gun and squeezed off a round. I watched astounded when his target's head exploded into a purple mist.

Jekto grabbed two of the guards in each of his upper arms and slammed them together with a sickening splattering sound and dripping guts. They collapsed to the ground dead. He picked up their weapons in his lower two arms and wielded them like they were weightless.

Another guard charged me. I aimed and blasted him square in his mouth. Whatever purple goo was inside his head sprayed all over the fellow behind him. I fired three more rounds, and three dracnarians died. The first of my pistols was empty.

Slowhand bounded from one enemy to the next, swiping with sharp claws. A trail of bloodied tentacles writhed like injured vipers on the floor behind him. At first, I thought his attacks were random, but I noticed nearly all the bloody snakes had eyes on them. He was taking out his enemies by blinding them.

Ginn sprayed searing hot plasma on the nearest guards. "Down to forty percent charge," she said, and then she twisted the control nozzle, cursed, and shook her hand like she'd grabbed the wrong end of a branding iron. "Switching to targeting mode."

A dracnarian snuck behind Jetko. I tried to scream out a warning, but the big guy didn't hear me over the noise of the battle, and the squid-head struck Jetko in the back with its wand. Jekto wailed in pain.

I aimed a Colt at Jekto's attacker, killing the guard with a single shot. Jekto charged forward in rage and pain, leaving a trail of his own blood behind. He drove his golden horn into the belly of the nearest guard, impaling him. The guard's body slid down, covering the dichelon's rhinoceros face. Now he, too, was blinded, and he spun, wildly grabbing at anything within reach with his lower arms as his upper ones tried to push the squid-head off. It reminded me of watching a kid get his butt stuck in an outhouse hole. Lots of flailing and little progress.

But I had my own problems. Three guards surrounded me, working in unison, swinging their disrupters as they circled me. I dove right, rolling on my shoulder away from them. I killed the nearest one and moved on to the next. My second shot was off-center and only wounded my attacker, taking a tentacle off but not even slowing him down. I shot him again. One less bad guy.

A motion from my left and a glint of gold caught my attention, as a disrupter came swinging toward me. I knew I was too slow to stop it, and I prepared for my head to look like Jekto's back. Time seemed to slow down as I raised an arm to block. The dracnarian's head exploded before me, and the wand clanged to the ground. My heart felt like it was about to burst from my chest.

I snapped my head back. Ginn's rifle pointed in my direction. I mouthed "Thanks," but she'd already turned her weapon toward her next target, and she was like a killing machine, she'd take one shot and get a kill — every time.

In all the commotion, I'd lost count of how many rounds I'd fired. I knew I was down to just a few and didn't have time to reload. I decided to grab the wand. It was well balanced and weighed about five pounds. I didn't know if I had to do anything to make it disrupt, or if it worked on impact. I clubbed the nearest squid-head with it but he barely reacted, and I caught no signs of disruption, just what I'd call annoyance. Perhaps I had it set on "melancholy distraction" mode instead?

Fine. I pointed my pistol at him and released the thunderous sound and destruction of a Colt .45. He had the courtesy to die right quickly, and I like to think while in a downhearted and preoccupied spirit.

The room was littered with dead dracnarians, the floor slippery with ooze and blood. Jekto still struggled with the carcass covering his face. My eyes met Rhuldan's, and I pointed toward the dichelon. "I'm going to try to help him," I said. I couldn't be certain he heard me, but he understood my intention, and followed, protecting my backside.

"Calm down! Let me help you!" I said, dodging his flailing arms.

"You're still alive?" Jekto asked.

"Yes. Now lower your head and hold still for a second. Rhuldan is covering us."

Jekto slowed his flailing and bent down. I grabbed several tentacles and pulled with all my strength, but the corpse was stuck good.

"I need to get some leverage," I said placing my boots on the big guy's knees and pulling, using my back and leg muscles. *Sloop.* The dracnarian's guts released their vacuum grip on Jekto's horn. I fell to the ground, covered in purple goo, some of which got in my mouth. It had a bitter, acidic taste with just a hint of ginger.

As I struggled to my feet, Rhuldan kept guards from getting close to me, while Ginn and Slowhand continued to fight. I snapped my head around to make certain I wasn't about to get hit.

Jekto roared a fearsome battle cry. Fueled by bloodlust, he charged directly at the Kraken. A few guards stepped in his way to stop him. I tried to take one of them out to the sound of a click coming from my pistol. *You're on your own, big guy.*

Jekto grabbed the guard on his right by several tentacles and spun him in a wide arc, driving him into the next nearest guard, knocking the second one dead into the wall. He tried to repeat the procedure to attack the third guard. I learned that dracnarian tentacles can't support stresses of supporting their entire body against centrifugal forces, so they snapped, sending it flying into the ceiling. The last guard stopped in his tracks, turned gray, and tried to run away, but Ginn's rifle ended his life in an instant.

Jekto continued attacking the Kraken, grabbing tentacles with all four of his arms and twisting them together as if tying knots. He pulled until they stopped moving, then grabbed two more pairs and did it again.

I found enough of a lull in the battle to reload one of my Colts and pocketed the spent brass casings while the Kraken screamed in agony.

Moby Dick's voice echoed in my ears. "Fools! You waste your time and energy killing my guards. We aspire to die in righteous battle as it only advances our great cause. The Holy Essence is long gone from this place!"

Slowhand raised his head, sniffing the air. "I smell treasure." He bounded off to a side room.

"Remember what we're here for," I called after him. He didn't respond, but I assume he either rolled his eyes or flipped me a one finger salute.

Moby Dick's skin darkened. "Treasure is of no importance to me. My reward awaits me in perfect balance."

I watched him closely, studying the colors and listening to his words, and I had my doubts. "Search everything. I think it's still here."

Slowhand yelled from the next room. "Jekto, how much can you carry? I've found their treasury!"

Jekto took a few steps, stumbled, and fell to the ground.

I raced toward the big fellow, and as I reached a hand toward him, surprised at the heat radiating from his body. "Is he supposed to be hot?"

Ginn said, "He's been fighting. We're all overheated."

"This is more than that. Let me see your back, Jekto," I said. His eyes fluttered, and he rolled over. The wound looked as if someone had cut out a pound of flesh, ran it through a meat grinder, and then slapped it back in place. It seeped a thick, brown liquid, but more concerning than that were the dark lines in his skin leading away from it. "It's his wound. It's poisoning him."

"Then there's nothing we can do," Ginn said.

I couldn't believe what she was saying. "What are you talking about? We have to help him."

"Not even the most trained doctors, using high carbon restraints and cliodepod tranquilizers will work on a dichelon. If we try to do anything with that wound, he'll kill us all in his dying rage."

"It's true, Idiom," Rhuldan said. "He's beyond help."

"I'm not going to just let him die here. Find me some alcohol. Whiskey, muldarian milk, whatever you have."

"Let it go," Ginn said. She pointed her weapon at Moby Dick. "You move, you die."

Slowhand called from the distance. "Hey, when you guys are done wasting time, I need help with this treasure. I can't carry it all." He carried a large bottle of liquid. "Here, Idiom. Drink yourself stupid. It's not a long trip." He tossed it to me. I pulled the top off and smelled it. It was definitely alcohol.

The big guy's breathing seemed faint and his eyes closed. "Jekto, stay with me."

"There's no dishonor in a battle death. Let me die."

"Sorry, I can't do that. I need you to drink some of this. Take about half of it." I handed him the bottle. He chugged it like it was a canteen of water and he'd been in the desert for days. "That's enough for now." I retrieved the bottle. "Now I need to do something, and I need you to show me the true warrior inside you. This is going to hurt, more pain than you've ever felt. I need you to remember that the poison in your system is your enemy and not me. Stay strong soldier, and you'll fight another day. Attack me, and we both die. Understood?"

"Yes."

"Control your rage. Fight the pain," I said. I pulled my bowie knife from my boot and poured some alcohol on it. "I'll work as fast as I can. Prove to me you're the bravest dichelon in the galaxy!" I plunged the knife into his wound, cutting out the disrupted flesh poisoning his body.

In my day, I've heard people scream. I've seen men get shot and shriek their last breath, and I've covered my ears at a woman's wailing from delivering a baby. But you haven't heard a cry like that of a dichelon having a fist-sized ball of flesh being cut from him. Blood-curdling wasn't the half of it. He screamed with an intensity that would scare bloodthirsty lions away from a freshly killed zebra. Several times I watched as his hands clenched into fists, and he fought to keep control. It was clear he wanted to kill me good, but somehow he fought back his urge to rip my limbs off.

I cut out all the bad flesh and scraped the wound clean until the blood flowing from it was more orange than brown. I dumped the remaining alcohol into the wound and packed it with some white cloth Rhuldan had found. Pointing toward a tapestry hanging from the ceiling, I said, "I need that," I said.

Ginn didn't reply, but she grabbed the cloth and yanked on it, sending the rod that held it clanging to the floor.

I cut the tapestry into several strips and tied it around him to hold everything in place. Jekto's eyes fluttered and finally closed. "Get some rest, big guy."

I noticed my hands shaking, and I wished I'd saved some of the booze to soothe my nerves.

Slowhand stood next to me and handed me another bottle. "Here. That was a stupidly brave thing to do."

"Hopefully he can recover. Did you find the element zero?"

"It's not here. We've searched everywhere. The one you call Moby Dick says it was removed by a team hours ago."

"I can't believe it's gone."

"I have a nose for valuable things. It's not here."

"Then this was all for nothing?"

Slowhand's eyes lit up. "For nothing? I found their treasury. There's enough here for us to pay off our debts and be set for a few years, even if we were to split it evenly. Of course, I'm the one to find the treasure, so I should get an extra share. Not to mention you're not really from around here. What do you have to spend money on? Since I'm the one who put Sarge together and he doesn't need coin, I should get…"

"We'll talk about this later. Do you think the base has taken out the dracnarian ships? I haven't felt any earthquakes lately."

Slowhand curled his upper lip. "Felt any what?"

"Tremors. They've died down."

"Oh yeah. In the heat of battle, I'd forgotten about that. Must have finished the…" Before he could complete his sentence, the moon shook with a massive explosion. Walls cracked, and everything shifted toward an odd angle. "That's a sign we better get out of here!" Slowhand bounded off, carrying a crate of treasure. Rhuldan and Ginn both were filling their packs with what they could take as well.

I began to follow him, but something stopped me. Moby Dick. *I can't believe he'd stay behind while the E.Z. was removed from here. He acted as if it was his own prize. I wonder...* I walked toward the massive dracnarian, held my breath, and laid my hands on him.

The universe opened up to me once again. Dust clouds formed into stars and ignited fires that burned for millions of years. I forced myself to remove my hands, falling to my knees. I caught my breath and called out. "The element zero is right here, team."

Considering the fact that the sphere of element zero was significantly larger than Moby Dick's mouth, I really didn't want to figure out how he had gotten it inside his body, but that's where we found it. Ginn and Rhuldan both fired several shots into his head to put him out of his misery, and I got busy cutting. After operating on Jekto, slicing open the massive dracnarian seemed an odd combination of disgusting and interesting. Purple ooze ran for a while and then gelled. My knife struck something too hard to cut through, and I pulled back the flesh. The black orb was wedged behind flexible ribs. I stabbed and sliced through them until the sphere rolled out on the floor, glistening in goo.

Jekto stood and walked carefully toward me. "I'll get this, my friend." He grunted in pain as he lifted the ball of element zero. "Now let's get to the ship."

Rhuldan had put his cloak and hat back on and carried a crate presumably filled with valuables. "It's time to leave."

"Grab that!" Slowhand said, as he pointed to a pack filled with credits. I flung the bag over my shoulder, and we marched back toward Sarge, my legs burned and shook with each step. I kept up with the others, noticing Ginn's legs quivering as well.

The common area, not long ago filled with civilians and commerce, now looked like a war-zone with goods and rubble spilled into the street and fires breaking out in multiple areas. Noxious, black smoke blurred our vision, making our passage more difficult, and caused my throat to burn. I coughed as dust filled my lungs, and Slowhand sneezed a high-pitched squeal, sounding like a long whistle.

A tremor shook everything, and debris peppered us from above. "Ginn, hurry!"

I followed her toward the docking bay. When a rock the size of my foot landed on his back, just inches away from his wound, Jekto screamed. I sighed in relief when we finally entered the docking bay.

Sarge yelled at us as we approached. "Double-time it, soldiers! We're under attack, and I don't enjoy waiting around for your pansy asses! Get up that ramp before I shoot you myself!" Hearing his voice was a strangely comforting sound, especially since I knew he didn't actually have any weapons.

Fayye stuck her head out Sarge's door. "Hurry! It's not safe!" Her eyes were wide, and her hands shook as she talked.

Ginn grabbed one of Jekto's hands to help him aboard. He looked a pale gray color, and he staggered, carrying the sphere of element zero. "We'll put that in a transport pod for storage." She opened an interior side hatch and detached a sealed container from its docking system. The entire unit seemed to magically float without support.

Meanwhile, Sarge's engines were spooling up for launch as the overhead hatch opened. Another strike hit the moon. The ship rocked.

Ginn opened the top of the pod. "Set it in there. Now, remember, Jekto, this pod number is 4A. Just don't use this pod when you need to defecate; got it?"

"Yes." Jekto's eyes fluttered as he released the large ball. "I'm going to rest now." He leaned against the wall and closed his eyes.

I leaned in close to the big guy to see if I could hear him breathing. He released a loud snore, and I smiled. "I think we made it."

As Sarge was just clearing the docking bay doors, his voice boomed from the speakers. "Brace for impact, we've got incoming debris! It looks like half a daemon is falling right toward us. Taking evasive maneuvers. Strap in, the chance of complete circumvention is zero point three percent!"

Ginn grabbed a seat and cinched up multiple belts. I did the same. An impact caused everything to spin sideways. A rush of wind and the sound of metal bending, filled my ears and overwhelmed my senses. How could I help? I held my breath and placed my hand over the Bible in my duster's breast pocket. *If it's time to take me, Lord, please make it quick and mostly painless.*

James Peters

CHAPTER FIFTEEN
AN UNEXPECTED STOP

Rhuldan leapt into action, grabbed an emergency repair kit from a bulkhead, ripped it open, and unfolded a large, thin sheet of nearly clear paper. When he snapped the material taught, it turned blue from the outside in. Ginn released her belt and helped him. Together they kept the paper from folding onto itself and from being sucked out into the vacuum of space. Their patch stuck in place, expanding outward like a bubble where the hull was broken away at the rear corner. I gasped for air. The ceiling spun wild, and I couldn't see.

Ginn grabbed a cylinder roughly the size of a loaf of bread. She broke off the top and pulled the trigger, spraying a black liquid to cover the patch. "Sarge, get us under control, now!"

Sarge didn't respond.

Ginn hit a red button, and strange, glass-fronted masks dropped from an overhead panel. She strapped hers on.

I grabbed a mask and struggled to pull it over my head, snapping stretchy bands into the back of my head. I positioned the clear part over my eyes and tried to take a breath. I began to panic when I realized I wasn't getting any air. Fumbling with the mask did nothing, and I flailed my arms. Ginn tapped me on the shoulder and flipped a switch on the side of my mask. Warm air pressure blew against my face. I took in several deep breaths, and as I did, the dark clouds faded away from my eyes. Ginn, Rhuldan, and Fayye stared at me. They each wore masks with glass fronts.

"Are you still with us?" Ginn asked. Her voice sounded strange through the transceiver thing in my ear.

"Yes, I'm better now."

"You need to learn how to use the emergency systems. One of us won't always be here to watch after you." Ginn's voice sounded strangely maternal.

"Thanks," I said.

"Sarge, can you hear us?" Ginn asked. Still no answer. "I'm going to the cockpit. If Sarge is out of commission, we're flying blind."

I was dang curious what she was going to do, so I followed her. I rolled my eyes when I saw Slowhand was still sleeping as if nothing had happened. Ginn sat in the pilot's seat and frowned.

"What's wrong?" I asked.

"Sarge is completely offline. I hope we didn't lose him. Put a mask on Solondrex while I fly this ship."

I strapped a mask designed for his furry, fat face over him, flipped the switch, and watched as the seals expanded. Slowhand snored but never moved. "He's set."

"If I know Solondrex, he'll be comatose for a week after working that hard on the moon. I need to find somewhere we can land this ship and try to make it space worthy. Leave your mask on until we have adequate pressure and oxygen. I can divert some waste gas from reaction mass into air. It's not the best for us, but it's better than breathing vacuum." Ginn busied herself with the controls, stopped, and said, "Idiom. You did good back there. I don't understand your motives and I don't always agree with what you choose to do, but today, I think you made the right choice, even when we didn't make it easy."

Am I getting enough air? Did she just say something nice? "I appreciate that, Ginn."

Ginn smiled for an instant behind her mask. "You should check on the others while I'm working."

I nodded and walked back to the main passageway.

Fayye touched my hand. "Are we going to make it? It would be terrible if we recovered the element zero only to die out here in space."

There was something about her words that gave me pause. I saw a tightness in her jaw and her eyes refused to meet my own. *Was she scared, or was she hiding some other emotion?* "Ginn's got it under control. Is Jekto still alive?"

"He is. We didn't have a mask to fit him, so he's just got an air hose in his mouth. I'm not even sure he needs it."

"I'm going to check on him."

Rhuldan tried spraying some medical foam on Jekto's wound, and the big guy was not having any part of it.

"Get away from me with that stuff," Jekto growled, trying to grab Rhuldan's hand.

"I need to treat your wound."

"I'm fine. Go away."

I rushed over to them. "Let's calm down. How's your back, Jekto?"

"It hurts constantly."

"I understand. One time I got bit by a snapping turtle. The bastard took a chunk out of my lower leg. It hurt for weeks. The worst part was having the doctor work on it. I swear I thought he was just trying to hurt me," I said.

"You should have let me die. At least I'd die in battle, not from infection."

"I felt the same way. But after the doctor was done, the pain began to fade. In just a few days, I was walking fine and only hurting if something touched the wound. After a couple of weeks, no pain at all, but I had a scar I could brag about. You trusted me well enough to work on you on that moon. Trust me now, and I'll do my best not to hurt you any more than is needed."

Jekto turned away from me. "You're lucky I didn't kill you."

"I know that. But you knew I was helping, and you were the bravest soldier I've ever seen. They'll be telling stories about how you mastered pain to control your rage in order to fight again another day. That's something to be proud of."

Jekto's chest puffed out. "You are right. I did master my pain, like no dichelon before me ever had."

"Now we need to work on you just a little more. Once we're done, you'll be good to go, right, Rhuldan?"

Rhuldan nodded. "Yes. Idiom's field dressing was impressive, but we need to finish the job with the medical kit. This spray will numb the area and sanitize it. Then we need to pack it with healing gel. It's going to feel better as soon as we're done."

Jekto's eyes squinted tightly. "If it doesn't, I'm going to be angry."

"Nobody wants that," I said, approaching him. "The worst part will be over soon. But first, I'm going to cut the tapestry holding the packing in." I pulled my knife from my boot and made the cut. "That wasn't so bad, was it?"

"No."

"Now this is going to be the worst part." I grabbed the blood-soaked cloth and pulled it off quickly. Jekto jerked and screamed, raising his golden horn up high enough to hit the ceiling. His eyes met mine with evil intent. "Hold on there, big guy. You'll be showing off your scar to the female dichelons in no time."

Rhuldan sprayed the wound with a yellow mist. "That should numb the area."

"It's better," Jekto grunted through clenched teeth.

Rhuldan bent a tube until something inside it broke. "Now for the healing gel." He pressed a button on top of the cylinder, filling the area with a white foam. He pointed the medical case toward the wound, and a bright blue light traced around the injured area, leaving a series of alignment marks. He pressed a button, and a perfectly shaped bandage was ejected from the case with the same targets. Rhuldan placed the bandage in precise orientation, and it sealed itself.

"How's that?" I asked.

"Not bad. It's mostly numb, but a little itchy around the outside."

Rhuldan sealed up the kit and returned it to its place on the wall. "Get some rest. You should heal up fine."

I took a few minutes to clean up and treat some of my own wounds, which were limited to a lot of bruises and a few scrapes. All in all, I'd been pretty darn lucky.

A few hours and a meal later, we all met in the Situation Room with the exception of Slowhand. I got the impression from Ginn trying to wake him would be fruitless and possibly deadly.

Ginn stood at the front of the room; all eyes were on her. "Everyone needs to know our status. The atmosphere in here is at an acceptable level, but I'd recommend keeping your masks with you. The patch is holding for now, but it won't survive a Null Space jump, so we're limited to Trad-Prop. We are three days from Gulliard, a primitive planet in the Rokulda system. I've run several simulations, and I believe we can survive a very gentle landing there."

Rhuldan took a sip from a steaming mug. "By very gentle, I take it you mean to use a lot of fuel."

Ginn nodded. "For us to land without breaking apart, we'll use nearly all our supply. I'm confident once Solondrex wakes up, he can fix the ship. But we won't have fuel to launch again."

Jekto leaned against a bulkhead, moving side to side against it, scratching. "How primitive is this planet? Can we buy fuel pellets there?"

"According to our databases, no higher-level life forms are native there, and there are no known outposts in the area."

Fayye coughed. "I have some favors I can call in. I should be able to get a transport diverted there. Of course, there's a cost involved."

Ginn's eyes tightened, and her nostrils flared. "There's always a catch with you, isn't there?"

Fayye returned the hateful scowl. "You can't expect a ship to alter course, land, and give us a good portion of their fuel for free."

Ginn crossed her arms, her muscles flexing as she spoke. "I suppose you'll want a cut of that money as a finder's fee?"

"Of course not. I just want to get the element zero back into grinkun hands where it will be safe."

Safe? None of us are safe from what this thing can do. If the dracnarians learn we've returned this to Fayye's cousins, they'll simply attack there in an effort to retrieve it.

"Do you have something to say, Idiom?" Ginn asked, apparently noticing my contemplation.

"Just sounds like we have little choice. We have to land somewhere, and I trust you considered all the options."

"Using Trad-Prop, that planet is our only option," Ginn said.

I nodded. "Ma'am, to me it sounds like our decision is made."

I sat in the cockpit as we approached the planet, not because I was of any help; I was just dang curious to see it from space. A violet colored planet slowly grew in size before us. A single moon appeared as we got closer, and I had a moment of hope this was Earth, perhaps from space it had a purple tint? They could drop me off and go on their way, and I could live out my life trying not to worry about what happens to the universe. That hope faded away as another, larger moon rose from behind the planet.

Ginn slowed us as we continued to get closer to the planet, saying, "We'll all burn up and die a horribly painful death if we used standard reentry protocols." I sat there for hours watching as details slowly appeared in the landscape. Just as I was about to close my eyes for a bit, Ginn made an announcement over the ship's communicator.

"We're now entering the mesosphere. Masks on, everybody. That patch is made for exterior vacuum, and I expect it to fail once pressure is equalized."

I put on my mask while she checked Slowhand's. Other than an occasional snore, he hadn't moved in days. I felt a vibration in my seat as we continued our approach. The shaking continued until it became hard to focus on anything inside the ship. The ship lurched and bucked like a fish trying to get from the shore to the water. "What happened?"

Rhuldan said, "The patch is gone, and some of the interior panels are starting to give way."

"Hold on to something," Ginn said. "I'm going to alter our orientation." She twisted a control handle, so we were no longer directly facing the ground and were now approaching it at an odd angle. "Is that any better back there?"

"Yes. The buffeting has slowed some," Rhuldan replied.

"Inform me if you see any structural failures," Ginn said.

I turned my head sideways toward her. "What are you going to do if we have a structural failure?"

"Brace for impact."

"That's not exactly the response I was hoping for."

"You asked."

We dropped fast for a moment as something changed in the air. Perhaps the wind had changed direction or suddenly thinned. All I knew was I felt my gut up in my chest, and I wanted to scream. Maybe I yelled a little.

Ginn adjusted some controls. "This planet's atmosphere is turbulent, and Sarge has the aerodynamics of a brick. It should get better as we get lower."

I realized my hands were gripping the arms of my chair like I was trying to gut a turtle by squeezing its shell. I forced myself to relax my grip. The ground grew closer, and I began to make out vegetation, mostly red and purple in color. Huge ruddy trees dotted the landscape, but we were headed to a clearing with only small shrubs and grasses. The ship shimmied and shook. Ginn stayed busy doing something with the controls. My mind raced, wanting me to do something, yet I knew there was nothing I could do. It seemed to take hours before we were ready to land, but in situations like this, it's difficult to estimate time.

Ginn set Sarge down more gently than I had expected. There was no sudden crashing or major jolt, just a sense of lunging forward a bit as we landed. I took several deep breaths. Ginn unfastened her seatbelts, stood, and glanced at me.

I released my seatbelts. "I'd ask if all landings are like that, but something tells me you'd just say 'No, some of them are rough.'"

Ginn shook her head. "Seems like you've already heard a bit of pilot humor. Let's check on the others and survey the damage."

CHAPTER SIXTEEN
DEALING WITH PRIVATEERS

I learned Planet Gulliard was at a stage where plants were the primary lifeform and oxygen levels were high—very high by my standards. I'd need to be careful with fire and keep my mask with me in case I noticed vision issues or dizziness. I'd have never guessed too much oxygen could be a problem.

The damage to the ship was limited to the upper part of his left rear corner, but a good-sized chunk had been torn away. Our main concern, however, was the damage to Sarge. His connections had been severed, so we weren't able to determine if we'd lost him. It occurred to me how strange it was that I felt a sense of sadness for the loss of a disembodied voice. Even without a proper body, he was Sarge and I could talk to him. I thought of him as part of the team.

Ginn almost convinced me that Slowhand could fix the ship once he woke up, but I caught a twitch in her eye when she said it, and she didn't mention Sarge, just saying "the ship." Meantime, we needed to scout the area, bring back any supplies we could find, and search for any dangerous beasts.

Fayye insisted on privacy while she called to have a transport diverted our way. Jekto wanted to explore an ever-expanding perimeter, and after a few minutes I decided to follow him. I was awestruck at the alien blue soil and purple trees with strange, glowing tips that swayed, snake-like against the wind. Wispy clouds made the red sun glow as if it were always sunrise. My mind raced thinking about what creatures might appear at any time, so I walked faster than normal until I caught up with the big guy.

"Finding anything good?" I asked.

"Earlier I found a slimy newt creature the size of my finger."

"Do you think it was the most advanced creature living here?"

"I don't know. It tasted like Jheldion mudskipper. Maybe a little muddier."

"How's your wound?"

"It hurt when I bent over to pick up the newt."

"Sorry to hear that. Do you trust me, Jekto?"

He stopped his walking and turned directly toward me, tapping my nose with his horn. It made my eyes water, but I tried not to flinch. "You are puny and know nothing, but you have the heart of a warrior. I trust you."

"Thanks. I trust you as well. Speaking of trust, what do you think of Fayye?"

"That one stayed on the ship while we battled. She hasn't earned trust from me."

I nodded. "I have my reservations as well. Have you ever heard of the shell game?"

"Yes. The finest warriors from all the tribes meet at the obsidian beach to smash each other over the head with the shells of giant kerithans. First one to knock out an opponent wins. Great fun!"

"I had a different shell game in mind, and I need your help."

"I will help you and look forward to smashing someone with a shell."

I told him about my plan. He didn't seem to understand, but he agreed anyway.

On the second day on the planet, Rhuldan discovered a cave with a deep natural spring inside it. The water was clean, but Ginn insisted we were to filter it before drinking or cooking with it. I actually had valuable skills here and found an outcropping of red and blue tubers that could be boiled and made edible. It reminded me of the conversation I'd had with Ginn so long ago before all of this happened. She made no mention of it, so I let it go. The roots made me think someone had dropped a filthy saddle in a cookpot, but they were filling. Honestly, I'd had worse food.

Jekto had filled up several transport pods with his dropping, so I offered to help him dump them. We took them to the cave and cleaned the storage units out with the water. Although he hadn't lied about his waste, he made perfectly round, large pellets as hard as granite, and they had no odor to them. I had to laugh when he explained how they'd used them to pepper the dracnarian daemons, and how one had even pierced through a window, causing an entire section of the ship to decompress. Normally I'd be more concerned over the potential loss of life, but they were out to destroy everything. Serves them right.

Fayye called us all into the Situation Room. "I've contacted a privateer who's willing to bring us a case of fuel pellets in exchange for some of the treasure you recovered."

"Isn't privateer just another name for a pirate?" I asked.

"Of course it is," Jekto said. "How much of the treasure do they want?"

Fayye replied, "It amounts to about ten percent."

Jekto raised his upper arms in protest. "We risked our lives to get that! Now they want ten percent just to bring us fuel?"

Fayye shrugged. "They're not going to do it for free. I can cancel the deal if you have a better solution."

I crossed my arms as my gut told me this could get dangerous. "We need to hide the ship and make the exchange away from it. I don't know these particular fellas, but privateers tend to strike when they see weakness, and with a damaged ship, we're not in a position of strength. Ginn, did you save the rifle I gave you back on Earth?"

Ginn looked at me as if I were crazy. "Yes. Aft storage compartment."

"Good. We're going to need it."

"Do you think this is going to turn into a firefight?"

"The way I see it, prepare for the worst and hope for the best. While I was out scouting, I found a place that might just work. There's a valley a few hours from here, with high ground on both sides. I'll find a place to provide me cover and a good clean shot toward the meeting spot. You'll do the same, Ginn. Jekto can bring the payment with him and meet up with them to make the exchange. I imagine the sight of a dichelon will encourage them not to try anything, but if they do, we'll cover the big guy."

Rhuldan nodded. "Many races fear the sight of my kind as well. I'll join him."

I stroked my chin. "No. I need you to sneak around to the other side, in case they try something dirty."

"What do you think they'll try to do?" Rhuldan asked.

"I'd expect them to pull a slimy trick like putting guns in the high ground to cover the hand-off."

"I can only look over one side of the valley," Rhuldan said. "If Solondrex were to wake up, he'd be a help."

"We can't count on that. If you find a gunman on the hill, take him out and take his gun, then search the other side for another one. Do what you have to."

"If someone threatens me, I'll end their existence," Rhuldan said.

Jekto grunted. "I like ending things too."

I smiled at Jekto. "Only if they try to break the deal. If that happens, you're free to rip an arm off. But it's best to let them live, that way they'll tell all their buddies not to mess with Jekto."

Jekto mumbled, "I hope they try to break the deal."

"Meantime, we need to hide Sarge," I said.

Ginn turned her hands upward. "We have enough fuel to begin reaction, nothing more."

"And that means?" I asked.

"We can't fly Sarge anywhere," she replied.

"Does he have wheels underneath that belly of his?" I asked. "I'd have to imagine ships like that need to move on the ground as well."

"He does, but we don't have a tug here."

"Who needs a tug when you've got a dichelon?"

Even for Jekto, pulling Sarge was hard work. We connected heavy cables to tow hooks, and the big guy pulled with all his might while the rest of us pushed, moving about fifty feet before needing to rest. We repeated the process until we had the ship hidden under the thick canopy of yellow-barked trees with brown leaves larger than my head. We were lucky to find the grass native to this world was very resilient and straightened itself back up after just a few hours, hiding our path.

We placed what Ginn called a locator beacon in the valley where we wanted to meet, and Fayye contacted her privateers, telling them the frequency to search for. Jekto and I made a few more trips to empty storage pods while Ginn hunted for something large enough to feed us all. I didn't ask if she transformed into the beast as part of her hunt. I ate the lizard-like creature she returned with after cooking my piece thoroughly over a small fire. It tasted nothing like chicken.

Fayye exited Sarge and said, "Contacts will be here in approximately eight hours." She smiled and carried a tool in her hand. Parts of her face were covered in dirt. "They're going to leave us a crate to carry the fuel for a few more credits."

She went back inside, and out of the corner of my eye, Jekto kicked a rock and cursed. I shrugged and continued cleaning my Colts. Where was I going to get more ammo for these?

As expected, Fayye said she'd stay back with the ship and wait for us to do the work. Jekto glared at her, unblinking. He wagged a finger at her, and she shirked away and made herself busy.

I waved at him and mouthed, "Don't worry about her."

"If one credit is missing when we return, I will gouge my horn into her brain," Jekto said.

Ginn said, "The locks require at least three of our four codes to open. You've got nothing to worry about."

We walked toward a deeply cut valley littered with an occasional sparkling silver boulders that would blind me when the sun hit them just right. Jekto and I took point as Ginn and Rhuldan followed many steps behind us.

Jekto glanced back. He spat on the trail. "I do not trust that grinkun."

"Neither do I. Let's just stick to the plan. If she pulls something, you can get the first crack at her."

"If I take a crack at her, there will be nothing left for the rest of you."

"I believe you," I said. We continued on, until we were ready to get everyone in place. I touched Jekto's lower arm. "Keep marching straight on, while I climb that hill and get in place. Keep everything under control."

"I am master of my emotions. I am a warrior."

"Yes, you are. Remember our first choice here is to make the trade. If they try to rob us, only then can you rip off an arm. Got it?"

"Yes."

"Carry on. I'll contact you via comms when I get in place."

I noticed climbing the hill didn't tire me out as much as I expected, and I found climbing a tall tree with lots of thick branches to be easy, as if I weighed about half as much as normal. I had a great view of the valley and Jekto carrying the coin. Knowing his height, I made some adjustments to my sights. Then I thought about the fact I'd be aiming downward, and I wasn't sure about the wind. If I felt lighter than usual, what would that to do my rifle's aim?

I called Jekto. "Set the crate of money on the ground and step back a good bit. I need to zero in my sights."

"What are you going to do?"

"Just watch." I aimed at the stash of money, held my breath, and found that calm moment before the storm. I squeezed the trigger. The bullet hit the ground short and to the right of where I'd aimed. I made a couple of adjustments to the rifle's sights and took another shot. This one hit just inches short. I added a final tweak. "I'm good to go."

Ginn's voice rang in my ear. "What are you doing?"

"Had to adjust my sights. All set now. Do you need to do the same?"

"No. My rifle self-adjusts. Are you certain you can hit anything from that far away?"

"I'm confident. Have you found cover?"

"Yes."

"Do you have a clear view of the crate?"

"Perfectly clear," Ginn responded.

"Good. Sit tight." I pressed Rhuldan's name on my arm. "How are you doing?"

"I've found a location that will provide a clear view of the hand-off."

"Good. Stay hidden and listen for anybody approaching. If they are headed your way, they're up to no good."

"Just like us?" Rhuldan asked.

"We're the good guys, remember?"

Rhuldan's voice turned to a whisper, "I think I hear something. Going silent."

I watched as what looked like a pair of giant yellow grasshoppers carry a large crate into the valley. Light reflected off their large, compound eyes, shifting from purple to orange. They stopped and made a bowing motion toward Jekto. He carried the crate of money toward them, and opened the lid. One of the grasshoppers pulled something from his belt, and I trained my rifle on his head, ready to take the shot.

The grasshopper pointed his device toward the case of money and motioned toward the other one to grab it. Jekto stepped forward, blocking their path. He then circled the crate and read a gauge mounted in the lid.

"Everything look good, Jekto?" I asked.

"It's full."

"Then let's end this standoff. Grab the crate and walk away."

The grasshoppers walked past Jekto and picked up their treasure and began their retreat. After getting clear, I watched them stop and turn back toward Jekto. "Something's up!" I yelled out on the comms.

The crack of an energy weapon echoed from up high. I wanted to turn to look at the source, but I knew I needed to watch the two grasshoppers in the valley.

Rhuldan called on the comms. "Don't let them move. They've got the crate rigged to explode."

The bug on my side reached for something on his hip. I squeezed off my shot, the bullet ripped through his insect arm. The lower part of that limb fell to the ground.

Ginn fired as well, striking her target in the side. "What did you see, Rhuldan?"

"A lughelon was sneaking around on my side. He had a nice rail rifle equipped with an ultiscope, and a remote detonator on his belt. I snuck up behind him, grabbed his leg, and stopped his hearts. I trained his weapon on his counterpart across the valley. When that one reached for his detonator, I put a hole through his main neural cortex."

"Can I kill them?" Jekto asked.

"There's been enough killing today," I said. "Get their weapons and if they have detonators, get those as well."

"But you said I could rip their arms off," Jekto said.

I shrugged. "One arm."

Jekto held the two giant grasshoppers by their throats as the rest of us climbed down the embankments. By the time I arrived, they both were hanging limply, gasping for air. Two insect arms had been separated from their respective bodies—the one I shot off and one he had ripped off in anger.

I slung my rifle and drew both pistols, pointing at the giant bugs. "Gentlemen, or should I say gentle insects. We had a deal. You could have taken a good bit of coin with you and gone back to you grasshopper homes and bug families safe and sound. However, you decided you wanted more, so you broke the deal."

Jekto smiled a toothy grin. "You tell them, Idiom!"

Rhuldan added, "Don't hold anything back."

Ginn made a rolling motion with her hand as if telling me to go on.

My bravado grew, and I was feeling tough as horseshoe nails. "As I was saying, we don't take kindly to folks who break deals, and we're not the type of people you want to cross. Now, I'm going to give you an opportunity to apologize to us all and grovel for your lives. If, and I do mean *if*, I find your pleas heartfelt and remorseful, I *might* let you live."

Ginn cleared her throat. "Nice speech. Too bad they can't understand you."

"What are you talking about? Everybody here understands each other."

"These two are drones. They have no language skills or independent thought. Their queen gave them direct instructions, and they were to follow them. Had that container exploded, this entire valley would be a smoldering crater."

I stared into Ginn's eyes. "You mean they were on a suicide mission?"

"Yes."

"Then they didn't care about the money here. That would imply their queen had a bigger fish to fry."

Ginn's face contorted into a confused smirk. "You make no sense. Lughelon don't eat fish."

"It's a figure of speech. I mean they had a bigger deal. Since Fayye made that deal with them, it certainly suggests she's double-crossed us."

"Can I kill these two?" Jekto asked.

"Ginn, what will happen when they get back to their queen?" I asked.

"They are damaged. They will be brought to her, and she will consume them."

I glanced at Jekto, who had a slight grin on his big rhinoceros face. I said, "She can find her own damn food."

Jekto slammed the two bug's heads together, spraying slimy, mustard colored goo in the air. A big glob of it dripped from his golden horn.

Ginn handed him a small towel from her pocket.

"What?"

"Wipe your horn off. That's disgusting."

"I don't see anything."

"Trust me. It's covered with guts." Jekto just shrugged, so Ginn snatched the towel back, wiped off his horn, and flung the towel near the dead grasshoppers. "I'm going to see if I can detach the detonator from the crate. Their queen may have another remote."

Rhuldan was inspecting his new rifle. It had a tiny opening, similar to his pistol. "Nice find," I said.

"It's a rail rifle. Deadly and accurate. You can shoot it sometime."

"I'm looking forward to that."

Ginn studied the crate. "Good news. All they did was to toss in a remotely controlled detonator." She pulled out a device small enough to fit easily in her hand and walked toward Jekto. "How far can you throw this?"

"Let's find out." He threw the bomb further than I could throw a baseball. The device exploded like a stick of dynamite when it hit the ground.

We gathered up the credits, and began our trek back toward Sarge. At about the halfway point, Ginn startled and raised a hand. Everyone stopped and fell silent. A ship's engine roared in the distance, and we saw it rising over the trees from Sarge's direction.

Ginn's eyes flared in a furious rage. "That bitch!"

Rhuldan peered through his rifle's scope. "It's a migrun runabout. Do you want me to take the shot?"

My mind raced. "No!"

And of course, Ginn said, "Yes."

Rhuldan kept the ship in his sights. "I need an answer."

I raced toward him and pushed his weapon off target. "Let them go." We watched as the ship flew away, disappearing over the horizon.

Ginn grabbed my arm, her grip painful. "That was our one chance to stop that ship!"

"There's been enough killing today. We don't know exactly what happened until we get back to Sarge."

"Fine," Ginn said. None of us spoke the rest of the way back.

James Peters

CHAPTER SEVENTEEN
DOUBLE-CROSSED

When we got back to Sarge, I wasn't surprised Fayye had gone. Ginn ran to the storage hold to find pod 4A missing as well. This, too, didn't surprise me. What did surprise me was how she slammed me against the bulkhead, knocking the wind out of me. She pointed her plasma rifle directly in my face.

"Calm down, Ginn," I said.

Hatred brewed in her eyes. "Rhuldan had the shot. He could have brought them down."

The sound of a charging rhino thundered through the ship. Jekto ran toward Ginn as if he would impale her.

I had to stop him. "Jekto, stand down and remain silent." He grumbled and walked away. I looked directly at Ginn. "Now before you kill me, at least let me talk."

"Your talking is what got us into this mess. We'd all be better off just to leave you here."

"Don't forget, I was the one to come up with the plan to meet the privateers. We'd all be dead had I not planned that out."

"You got lucky, nothing more. The only reason we're here is because of you anyway."

"True, and we can argue all day long about what caused what to happen. But look at it this way: We didn't want the dracnarians to have the element zero because they wanted to destroy everything. Fayye double-crossed us. I'd bet ten silver dollars she knew all along that the squid-heads had stolen the ore from the migrun, and she had no interest in getting it back to her cousins. She was looking for a payday and perhaps a diplomatic favor from the migrun."

Ginn eased her grip on me just a little. "I don't doubt this, but I don't like being played the fool."

Sometime during our conversation, Rhuldan had entered and stood behind me. "I've thought about this on the way back. It was the right call not to take the shot. That ship was a small runabout, without jump capabilities. That means there is a bigger ship out here, close by. Had I taken the shot, they would have annihilated the entire area with warheads from orbit. It's for the best we let them have their prize and live to fight another day."

Ginn let go of me. "I thought you didn't want the migruns to have the element zero because they'll use it as a weapon?"

I straightened my shirt and knocked some dust off my jacket. "Yes, but a weapon to fight small battles as compared to destroying everything. It's the lesser of two evils."

Ginn slung her gun over her shoulder. "How is it you've come here and caused everything to go crazy?"

"I wish I could explain, but I don't have a clue. I'm hoping the dracnarian treasure we found is enough to cover our debts and make things straight."

"All the costs you've caused are coming out of your share."

"I know."

"Something doesn't make sense though. What caused the explosion in the docking bay back on Panadaras? I assumed it was the migrun, and they wanted to stop the team Fayye hired from taking back the ore. But if she was working with the migrun, it couldn't have been them."

I hadn't thought of that in some time. "We may never know. The way I figure it, those fellows made a lot of enemies over the years. Most likely, one caught up with them."

Slowhand approached, shuffling at a snail's pace. His fur was unkempt, and he yawned while one of his hands scratched his butt. "What did I miss?"

Trying to describe how Slowhand fixed the ship would be impossible because I couldn't understand it myself. He explained that all he had to do was to touch the pieces he needed to merge together, twist their molecules along the Z axis, draw them together and then allow them to return to their normal orientation slowly. The way he described it, it was something along the line of eating or breathing to him. Watching it happen, it looked more like magic, as pieces of the ship would disappear from sight and then reappear perfectly repaired. He had to work in some sections from one of the transport pods to replace lost material as well. All I can say is his work was exquisitely smooth and somehow looked to be square. He also claimed the repair to be stronger than the original structure, and nobody had any reason to question him.

Once Slowhand had fixed the ship, he needed another nap, this one lasting several days. Rhuldan and I scouted for any sign of a giant grasshopper queen's ship. We discovered signs of a landing on the other side of the valley, but the vessel had left. We hoped they'd cut their losses and learned a lesson not to mess with us, but we remained diligent and always covering our tracks.

I also got a chance to fire Rhuldan's rail rifle, and I'm here to tell you these people have got it made. It automatically adjusted for wind, change of elevation, distance, atmosphere, and even learned to adapt if you had poor control when firing. If you put the crosshair on your target and pulled the trigger, even a complete greenhorn could hit a bullseye.

Once Slowhand woke up again, he was ready to work on Sarge the AI, not the ship. He found a section of connecting fibers had been severed, and several power units had been destroyed. I have to hand it to the furry fellow, he salvaged a power supply and connectors from a storage pod, and even though they were of drastically different designs, he merged them together to make a repair. We all waited in the Situation Room as Sarge restarted.

"You are the most pathetic looking bunch of recruits I've ever seen! Look at all of you, out of uniform and standing there with extra arms and whatnot. You make me want to puke, go and eat again, so I can repeat the process!"

Ginn sighed and her face softened. "It's good to have you back, Sarge.

"Somebody give me a situational update, pronto!" Sarge demanded.

"We've landed and had to make repairs. There's no danger." Ginn replied.

"I'll be the one to say if it's safe or not! Why are we being scanned by a lughelon queen's ship?"

Ginn's eyes flared. "I'd hoped they'd left the system, but it seems they decided to remain."

"I'll take care of this," Sarge said. "Attention, lughelon ship! This is the migrun dreadnought *Zammarius*. You have exactly five seconds to cease your scanning before I launch a volley of fusion warheads precisely at your location. Do you understand me?"

A stuttering voice replied, "Our apologies, *Zammarius*. We were unaware of any other migrun vessels in the area."

"Then I'd recommend you find another location for yourselves to occupy. Noncompliance will be seen as an act of aggression. Missiles at the ready!"

"We're calculating a Null Space Conduit now. We want no trouble. We're jumping in three, two, one…"

"Are they gone?" I asked.

"Gone like a sailor's paycheck on the first day of shore leave," Sarge said.

Ginn's lips curled up in a rare smile. "Sarge, perform a complete system check in preparation for launch."

"Aye. I need an engineering team to report to reactor core for full inspection."

Ginn muttered quietly, "I'll work with him."

The ship lifted just off the ground enough to move out from under the tree line and then Sarge kicked in the engines. I felt as if I were being smothered by a concrete blanket as we left the primitive planet. The thrusting calmed as we exited the atmosphere, and strangely enough, I was relieved to get into space.

During the Trad-Prop portion of our trip, we spent the better part of a full day arguing over the distribution of the dracnarian treasure. Slowhand believed he'd earned at least half of it, Jekto threatened to kill all of us if he didn't get his fair share, and Rhuldan stared everyone down with a deadly look on his face. Ginn insisted she should get some additional compensation for her trouble with the migrun, and everyone (except for me, of course) agreed that the "incidental costs of this operation" should come from my share. By the time we were done, we had a formula written on a board in the Situation Room, complete with the letters and symbols I doubted Sir Isaac Newton could've comprehended. I ended up with the smallest stack of trilatinum credits. I should've fought for more, but we had some time to kill on the way back. I had a deck of cards, so I had a plan to redistribute the wealth in a more equitable manner.

I went to the cockpit to see Slowhand hanging upside down. He had one hand resting on a control panel; his gaze focused somewhere out in space.

"Hey." I stepped across the threshold.

He nodded.

"That was some battle back on the base. You surprised me. You moved like a cheetah with its tail on fire."

"You surprised me as well, you surviving and all."

"Yeah, I'm not as easy to kill as everyone assumes. So, what happens now?"

"We're headed back to Panadaras, where we'll allow you, Rhuldan, and Jekto to exit the airlock and hopefully we'll never see each other again."

I acted as if I were studying the displays, but in truth I was trying to buy some thinking time. "I was thinking about that. We're all stronger as a team. Perhaps we should all stick together?"

"Ha! Not a chance, biped!" Slowhand crossed his eyes and pulled his upper lip back to show me his teeth.

Ginn entered the cockpit behind me. "What's with the stupid face, Solondrex?"

"This idiot thinks we are a team and should all stick together!"

A smile curved across Ginn's face and then she burst out laughing, pointing at me. "You truly are insane, aren't you? You think we're a team?"

"I, uh…" I tried to respond.

Rhuldan had silently entered. "What's going on here?"

Ginn shook her head. "Idiom thinks we should all stick together once we get back to Panadaras."

"That's not going to work for me," Rhuldan said. "Considering how the migrun wanted to capture me for some nefarious purpose, I'm heading to more neutral territory."

"What's with the meeting?" Jekto wiggled his way into the cockpit, squeezing us all in so tightly we couldn't move.

Slowhand laughed, "Idiom here… wait, I can't say it," he laughed again. "He wanted all of us to stick together as a team!"

"He jokes! What fun," Jekto said. "Not me. As soon as I get back, I'm going to Dichel. There are a few hundred dichelon females who need to see my scar, among other things."

"So that's it? We get back to the base, and we all go our separate ways?" I couldn't believe this was it.

Everyone spoke at the same time. "Yes."

James Peters

CHAPTER EIGHTEEN
EPILOGUE

We made it back to Panadaras and docked in bay B163. Ginn and Slowhand settled up with the migrun authorities and prepaid for the next several cycles, so they and Sarge had a place to stay.

I collected my rifle and what little gear I had along with my now larger stash of trilatinum credits and said a quick farewell to Sarge, Ginn, and Slowhand. I'm not certain, but I thought I detected just a hint of sadness in Ginn's eyes before she turned away. She seemed to be busy, occupying herself with something that looked important, but I suspected wasn't.

I gave Rhuldan a hearty handshake, wishing him the best of fortunes. My stomach roiled as the sensation of time flip-flopping overcame me. "Until we meet again."

"That's an unusual thing to say," Rhuldan paused, then added, "perhaps we shall, Idiom."

Jekto was just about to leave, so I waited on him for a minute. "Hey, Jekto, walk with me." We exited the airlock. I scanned side to side to make sure nobody was in earshot. "Thank you for keeping your word."

Jekto took in a deep breath, puffing out his chest. "I promised to keep your secret by my code as a warrior. I suspect we did the right thing."

"I do too. Just remember, tell no one."

"Your secret is safe with me."

"Now go back to Dichel and show off that scar. Tell the women how brave you were and your kill count."

"Oh, no!" Jekto said, "I lost count of my kills!"

"Twenty-seven," I said, pretending as if I had actually counted them.

"Twenty-seven! That would earn me a medal in wartime!"

"Trust me; you've earned one."

I wasn't sure where to go, but I found myself heading down to the seedy bar deep below the common areas. The same green-skinned, frog-mouthed bartender was there, but he didn't seem to recognize me. I figured he saw so many different types of beings; a devilishly handsome human didn't make much of an impression.

"What will it be?"

"Something that didn't come out of another creature."

"Have you tried an Ionic Blaster?"

"Not yet. How much?"

"Two credits."

I set three coins on the bar. He reached under the counter, produced a glowing bottle, and poured a shot. It fizzed, sending millions of tiny bubbles into the air.

I sipped the drink and thought about everything. When I had realized Fayye would double-cross us, and how Jekto and I pulled the oldest trick in the book on the "team." You see, while we were dumping his droppings back in the cave on that primitive planet, we used his pride and joy: a ball of dung so large, it must've weighed fifty pounds. Together, we sprayed it with a can of black sealant I'd pocketed from Sarge's emergency repair kit, and we made the switch, putting that shiny black poo in storage pod 4A, in place of the element zero. We dumped that into the bottom of the deep underground spring, where it should be safe from prying eyes for many years to come.

Fayye and the migrun stole nothing more than a blackened dichelon turd from us. What happens to Fayye is her problem. I have no sympathy for her as she double-crossed the wrong man.

I finished the Ionic Blaster, and a sense of warmth flowed through my body. Would I ever see Rhuldan, Jekto, Ginn, Slowhand, and Sarge again?

I had a feeling I just might.

James Peters

ABOUT THE AUTHOR

James Peters fell in love with Science Fiction at a young age, becoming hooked on the works of Asimov, Anderson, and Pohl (among many others), as well as the mixed bag of anything labeled Science Fiction on television or at the movies while growing up. While in grade school, he was given an assignment to write a journal about anything he wanted. He quickly filled the pages with a Buck Roger's type adventure of robots, spaceships, and pew-pewing lasers, discovering his inner passion to write.

He writes with a gritty blend of character-driven action, wry humor, and social commentary that transports the reader through wild worlds of speculative fiction and fantasy. He's known to cross the borders of different genres into new territory, along with an occasional 'wink and nod' to pop culture and other authors, then shock the reader with an unexpected turn of events.

Sit back, open your mind and enjoy the ride. Your adventure awaits.

Psst – Idiom and the crew will be returning for more adventures.

If you enjoyed this book, please leave a review online. Reviews are like magical items to authors, providing them energy to continue writing and to level up so someday they can stand before the Balrog and say "You shall not pass" to save their party of mostly short adventurers.

Author's links:

https://www.amazon.com/-/e/B017TQ8VUS

https://www.facebook.com/BlackSwanPlanet/

https://www.goodreads.com/author/show/17190935.James_Peters

Made in the USA
Middletown, DE
30 October 2023